The Execution

Also by Robert Mayer

SUPERFOLKS

Robert Mayer

THE EXECUTION

THE VIKING PRESS   New York

First published in 1979 by The Viking Press
625 Madison Avenue, New York, N.Y. 10022

Published simultaneously in Canada by
Penguin Books Canada Limited

LIBRARY OF CONGRESS CATALOGING IN PUBLICATION DATA
Mayer, Robert, 1939—
The execution.
I. Title.
PZ4.M4692EX [PS3563.A954] 813'.5'4 78-13652
ISBN 0-670-30050-0

Printed in the United States of America

Set in Videocomp Century Expanded

This book is dedicated
to Max Mayer,
to the memory of Anne Mayer,
and to Betty Mothner

It is dark. I can hear wood, silence: I know them. But not living sounds, not even him. It is as though the dark were resolving him out of his integrity, into an unrelated scattering of components. . . .

WILLIAM FAULKNER
As I Lay Dying

The Execution

Walter Briggs

➤ He called the night they stole the city champs from us, and I wasn't home, and he called again the next afternoon, and I still wasn't home. Mama told him to come on up on Sunday afternoon if he wanted, which he did. He was wearing one of them powder-blue leisure suits, with his white collar flattened down over the lapels, and a choker of turquoise and shell. He had a good build and he didn't look more than thirty, but his hair was thin and his scalp was salmon-colored from the sun.

We sat in the living room with the blinds pulled up and the kids playing stickball in the street. Mama told Leroy to go out and play, but Mr. Peterson—that was his name—Mr. Peterson observed as how Leroy looked like he would be playing high-school ball himself in a year or two, so he might as well stay and listen. Mama shrugged, so Leroy sat in Pa's old chair and watched.

Mr. Peterson zipped open a leather case he had on his lap —not an attaché case, more like a leather envelope—and pulled out brochures and pictures of the campus. The sky was real blue and the mountains a faded purple in the distance, like a mirage. They would give me free tuition, he said, and free room and meals, for as long as I played varsity ball.

"What happens if he don't make the team?" Mama said, sitting in her rocking chair with her darning in her lap.

Mr. Peterson smiled his sweet smile that crinkled lines near his pale blue eyes.

"Mrs. Briggs," he said, "I saw Walter score forty-two points in the city champs at Madison Square Garden the other day, plus two more at the buzzer they took away from him,

1

that cost his team the game. I also saw him score thirty-seven against Boys High with Dickie Aldrin sticking to him like flypaper, and I saw him hit twelve straight jumpers against Taft. There's no way he won't make the team."

He got up from the soft sofa and kneeled by the rocking chair and showed Mama the pictures of the campus, and the catalogue that listed all the courses they had to offer. An excellent English department, he said, and tops in biology, in case I wanted to be pre-med. At the same time he handed me a catalogue. Stuck inside mine was a travel folder advertising downtown Las Vegas, with pictures from the show at the Stardust.

"I got to be honest with you, Mr. Peterson," I said. "Till last year I never heard of the University of Nevada at Las Vegas."

Mr. Peterson got up from where he was kneeling. You could tell he had once played basketball himself.

"That's true of most people, Walt," he said. "That's why we're building us a national championship team. Three years from now when we win the NCAA, everyone will know about us. And fellows who don't have your kind of ability will come out just to study medicine or law. That's how colleges use athletics these days—to build a reputation that helps everybody. That's why we want you, and Dickie Aldrin of Boys High, and Nate Brown of Erasmus. You've got to admit that's some nucleus of a team."

"Aldrin and Brown are goin' too?" I said.

"Just about signed, sealed, and delivered," Mr. Peterson said.

I told him I would have to think it over, and he said of course, and left the brochures with us, except the one from the Stardust, which he stuffed in the pocket of his coat. I got letters from Maryland and Virginia, but they didn't have purple mountains like that.

"You want to go so far away?" Mama said.

"I got to see the world sometime," I said.

When Mr. Peterson came to see us again two weeks later, I told him there was two things I wanted. I wanted them to fly Mama out there so she could see the campus and Las

2

Vegas. And them mountains. And I told him I wanted an air-conditioned car to drive around in out there. What the hell, *they* come to *me*. No harm in asking.

Mr. Peterson was wearing one of them western bolo ties this time instead of his choker. And smiled his eye-crinkly smile and said that was a fine idea, they certainly could fly Mrs. Briggs out with me to see the campus. Only right for a mama to know where her boy is at, he said. As for the car, he said, I got a right good business head—he talked a little southern when he was saying no—but there was rules against that by the NCAA and they had to 'bide by the rules. How would it look—a working-class boy from the Bronx showing up in a shiny new car? He waited a minute and fussed around in his leather envelope. Then he said, on the other hand it is a right big campus, and a fellow needs wheels to get around. What they might be able to do, he said, was scrape up a Honda bike for me to ride around on if I promised to say I saved up for it on my own. If anybody asked. And he winked the same way he winked when he slipped me the Stardust brochure.

Mama started rocking back and forth like she does when she doesn't like something. I waited for her to say her objection, but she didn't say nothing. So I said to Mr. Peterson, "You got yourself a deal," and he pulled out a letter of intent for me to sign. The socks a basket of snakes in Mama's lap.

The night before I was ready to leave in September, Mama pulled down a great box from the top of her closet wrapped in Christmas wrapping.

"It's three months till Christmas," I said.

"Don't make fun of last year's paper," Mama said. "Just open the box."

I tore apart the pink angels singing to baby Jesus, and let the pieces slide to the floor. Inside the box was a jacket I been glomming three months at Alexander's. Black leather with four zipper pockets, two of them diagonal, and an extra one on the shoulder. A hundred and sixty-nine fifty. I didn't say nothing, but put it on. I felt like King Shit.

"Mama, we can't afford this," I said.

"Your college money will go to Leroy now," Mama said. "I reckon you're 'titled to the jacket of your choice."

I leaned over and kissed her on the cheek. "You're the best mama there is," I said. Which she is.

The next day was summer warm, and I carried the gleamy black jacket in my left hand and my suitcase in my right as I walked down the carpeted tube to the plane bound for Vegas. The plane was crowded, every seat taken, with people in bright clothing going for vacation. Dickie Aldrin wasn't on the plane, nor Nate Brown neither. Aldrin went to North Carolina, and Brown to Marquette.

Simon W. Merton ➤ The defendant was wearing a checked brown sports jacket, a white shirt buttoned at the collar, and a tie. I am not one to put much stock in clothing, but his neatness always surprised me. It would have been easier if he had looked like a bum. Which is irrational, but God's honest truth.

"All rise," etc. the court clerk said, etc. "Judge Simon W. Merton presiding."

"That boy comes up today," Sarah had said over breakfast. "Doesn't he?"

I sipped my coffee and read the front page of the *Tribune* and didn't answer.

"What are you going to do?" she said.

I put down the paper and stood and put on my coat. "Sarah, my hands are tied," I said. "You know what he did. Don't rip my guts out."

The defendant stood straight before the bench, keeping his head high, looking curious and interested. Just like through the trial.

"Walter Briggs, do you have anything to say to this court before I once more pronounce sentence?"

"Only that I am innocent of this crime," he said.

I guess I had been hoping he would break down and confess and beg for his life. It wouldn't have saved him, but it would have made things easier.

"You have been found guilty of the charge of first-degree murder, by a jury of your peers," I said. "The Utah Court of Appeals has upheld that conviction. The United States Supreme Court has refused to review your case. Your sentence

5

of death has been delayed during this long process. There are no more avenues of appeal, other than clemency from the Governor. It is therefore incumbent upon me as the judge in this case to set a new date for your execution."

I made a show of checking the calendar on the bench. The date was already fixed in my mind. Sarah and I would be at the judicial conference in Hawaii.

"I hereby sentence you to be put to death by the sovereign State of Utah at seven o'clock in the morning of July fourteen next."

I had expected his knees to buckle. Or something. He didn't flinch. Until what I said next. It seemed to catch him by surprise.

"Under the laws of the State of Utah, you have the right to choose the method of your own execution. Death by hanging or death by firing squad."

"Choose?" he said weakly, and looked at me with his soft, deceptive brown eyes, and then at his attorney, as if to see if I was joking.

"You don't have to decide now," I said gently. "You have until two weeks before the date of execution to make up your mind. If you choose not to choose, the warden of the state penitentiary will choose for you."

His eyes rolled back in his head then. His legs seemed to quiver. He was no longer looking at me, but over my head, as if at a distant mountain.

His attorney squeezed his arm. She gave me a look. If looks could kill, they say. The bailiffs took him away.

Two reporters were lounging in the jury box. They hurried over to talk to the attorney. I banged the court adjourned. I was in no mood.

In chambers, surrounded by the leather books of civilization, I chewed a Rolaid. It didn't help. Something was calling me back out to that courtroom, as if his ghost were already prowling there. I peered out. It was empty. I went inside, still wearing my black robes, and stood where he had stood before the bench, looking up at the vacancy that was me. I read the lettering on the wall above. You tend not to notice it after twenty-three years of your back turned.

I went back to chambers. You can't put yourself in another man's shoes. It is not humanly possible.

The thing to remember is what he did. That's what I keep telling Sarah. Remember what he did.

Daralyn Kirk ► Colored lights brighting up the sky and quick wheels spinning and the little ball jumping like a crazy person and the men in yellow jackets pulling money chips in and pushing them out all red white and blue and beautiful ladies—real ladies!—with hair piled shiny and high and bells ringing and quarters and nickels and dimes falling out of the slut machines. Las Vegas gives me goose bumps all over. Not like Miami where the water rolls in and in and you could simply die of fat ladies on the beach.

But it ain't right what Pinky did. Going off with that classy lady and me stranded here with no ticket home and no place to stay and nothing but two rolls of nickels he left on the dresser. "For the slut machines," he wrote on a paper. "Ha ha."

Me asking the man in the hotel for a job to make some money so I could go home. "Show me what you do best," he says. No windows in his office, like that place with the nurses, but I have to show him with his door made of glass and anyone passing by could look in and see. When I stand up with my knees cricking and sticky running on my chin and the front of my best red satin dress all sticky too he says he has no jobs now but he'll call me when. I walk downtown where a sign says "Waitress Wanted" and serve cocktails till a man calls for room service. In the morning he gives me a card and says I could get a job there. Big Lil's, it's called, out on the highway. I give my cocktail money to the cabbie.

Nine days I stayed at Big Lil's, never once taking off the pretty blue nightgown she gave me, except during. It was soft and filmy, not like the starchy white ones the nurses give.

In between I stared out my window at the purple mountains waving heatwise far across the desert. The prettiest mountains I ever did see. Till some big fat man stinking of the bourbon beat me black and blue all over my face. That is not what I like. So I left them their nightgown folded neat and put on my red satin dress with the two dollars each they was giving me in the pocket, and climbed out the window in the night, and started walking down the highway in my heels, away from the brighting lights.

The sun come peeking over the mountains, whiting up the desert with orange rouge, and I thought I would get a hitch, someone pretty as me, but there wasn't many cars leaving town before breakfast time, and I must have looked a sight. Till this sweet black boy comes riding by on a big black bike and pulls off the road and turns his bike to face me on the gravel like a cowboy in the movies whoaing his horse.

"You need help?" he says.

"I just got to get someplace away from here," I say.

"Well, get on, then," he says.

I swing my leg and climb on the back of his bike. He makes to start the engine and then stops. He climbs off'n the bike.

"What did I do?" I say. Afraid he's changed his mind.

He takes off the black jacket he is wearing, all leather and zippery, and makes me put it on.

"You'll freeze, riding like that," he says.

We ride then, me hugging my cheek against his back, feeling sleepy and smelling all leather and warm and him. And car fart, from the gas. Peeking backward every other minute at the long skinny highway behind. Afraid Pinky heard I had runned away. Afraid I'd see Pinky coming round the bend.

Walter Briggs ➤ The courtroom was dim and the

street was bright and the van was dark and the yard was bright and the cell is dim again. It gave my eyes a headache. Like when we were kids and went to the Loew's Post Road to see cowboy movies on Saturday afternoons and eat Goldenberg's Peanut Chews. And came out from the dark and it was still bright. It made you sneeze, too.

Choose.

I got the shot off in time, I swear it. I could have gone in for the lay-up, but there wasn't time. So I stopped short and pumped up the jumper from twenty feet. Rolled it sweet off my fingertips and knew it was good the second it left my hand. And the crowd screaming and the buzzer going off somewhere underneath and the cords leaping up clean and true. And everyone mobbing me and messing my hair, all sweat and teeth. And then confusion, and disbelief. The ref saying the buzzer went off first. Me screaming at him, the coach screaming at him. Someone pulling us away. Hustling me away to the locker room.

That's what started it. The whole thing. Funny, when you look at it like that.

"They set a date?" Jonesy said.

Jonesy is in the cell across. He gets it in three weeks. Maybe two.

"July fourteenth."

"Bastille Day," he said.

Jonesy killed three people while holding up a diner. That's what they say. I never asked him.

"Hey, Jonesy," I said. Trying to keep my voice sounding strong. "They tell you you got to choose?"

"Choose what?"

I don't want to upset him. But what the hell.

"You know. How you . . . get it."

"Oh, that. State law. They got to let you choose. Nice guys, the Mormons, eh what?"

He lights up a butt. He's got thick arms, with tattoos on both. A scorpion and a flower.

"Don't sweat it, kid, there's no choice. You got to go firing squad."

I'm getting a little sick. I keep it down. I keep talking.

"Why's that? I was thinking the other . . ." Would hurt less, I was going to say.

"You don't want to hang," he says. "Hanging they got to break your neck. If they don't, you hang there and suffocate. It takes too long. You shit and piss where everyone can see. Who wants to go like that?"

I nod. I struggle to keep the upchuck down in my chest. Maybe my headache wasn't from the sun.

"With the firing squad, they just lean you against the wall, and bang, it's done. You just make believe you're still in the war."

"Yeah," I say.

I was too young for the war.

I sit on my bunk and look at the black circles where the steel bars disappear into the floor.

Forrest Stone ► It was his, all right. I even handled it myself the night before.

They roared up on a black Honda at six o'clock, just as I was locking the glass doors of the Visitors' Center.

"Sorry, we're closed," I yelled out.

"How 'bout the campground?" he called back.

I walked down the stone steps toward them. That's when I noticed the bruises on her face. Dark blue, real welts. Never understood why some women go for that. And stick with the guy after.

I gave them directions to the campground two miles in off to the left. Not yet crowded in May. And saw the scabbard on his belt. The handle set with turquoise.

"That's a sweet-lookin' blade," I said. "Can I have a look?"

Not sure why I asked. I am a fancier, but it was more a premonition. After those welts. He unbuckled and handed it to me. I pulled it out of the sheath. The blade a good six inches, and razor-sharp. Never used, it looked to me.

"I bought it yesterday in Vegas," he said. "I'll be camping all the way to New York. I figured I ought to have a knife."

I nodded and sheathed the blade and handed it back to him.

"Most folks carry a pocketknife," I said.

He looked at me and said nothing, and I said nothing back. He buckled the knife on and revved his motor, and they roared off into the park.

Later I was having dinner at Lucky's Inn and the bike roared up and they came in and ate in a booth. Pork chops, I think. They didn't talk much. Hardly a word throughout. I must admit that Grace and Lucille were cockin' their ears to

12

pick up any trace. What with the welts and him being black, I suppose. The old folks who grew up out here aren't as liberal as some of us. I have to admit that.

I left before they were finished. I guess they went back to the campground later on. I shouldn't say I guess, though. I mean, it's a fact.

Josephine Briggs ➤ Ain't nobody that cares.

That's the most troublesome burden. They gonna put my boy to his grave for something he didn't do, and there ain't nobody pays no mind. Time was when folks cared about folks. I remember one time when I was flapping pigtails my grandaddy got his foot caught in the mowing machine. The doctor come and take off his leg. Nobody could do nothing, but folks came and brought cakes and candies and fruits. And they finished the mowing for him so he wouldn't lose his place. They was neighborly, back then. Now? Nothing. What's on the TV tonight. That's all they wants to know. And my Walter moldering on that Death Row, and nobody even asks. I guess they is too embarrassed.

He didn't do what they say, Reverend, you know he didn't. He ain't never been in trouble in his entire life. He tole me on the phone he didn't do it, right then. Don't worry, Mama, he said, the courts will find the truth. That was two years ago he said that. He believed it, too. And now they is gonna kill him, and they still ain't found the truth. My Walter just couldn't do something like that. That mutil . . . what they say.

"I think we should go inside and pray, Mrs. Briggs," the Reverend said.

We went from his office past the butcher shop to the church next door. The church was dark and candlelit, and we kneeled on our knees before the main altar, Jesus on the cross and Mary crying underneath.

"Dear God," I said, "Sweet Jesus, loosen the heart of the one that did it. Loosen his heart in your wisdom, and let him that did it come forward and tell the truth, before they kills

14

my boy. For that is the only way now. Let he who did it speak forth, for that is what would be right, under God."

"Dear God," the Reverend said, "have mercy on Walter Briggs in this time of his tribulation, and ease the burden in his heart, and cleanse his soul. So when in Your infinite wisdom You take him to Your breast . . ."

"No!" I scream. And stand up from my knees and look down at the Reverend looking up from his bowed head. "That's no fit prayer!" And run down the aisle on my bad ankles and out the big doors into the bright sunlight which blinds, and down the stairs. I start to cross the street, but my ankle twists on the curb and I fall to the gutter, heavy on my knee and my arm. The crosstown bus rushes by too fast to stop, a yard from my head, blowing hot bus breath in my face.

A fat man helps me up. "You all right?" he says. "It's a good thing you fell or that bus would've hit you sure. Jesus must've been lookin' down." He is wearing a white apron, with blood all over.

Virgil LeFontaine ➤ I take the bus marked Desire.

(Tourists find it quaint, and take photographs in front of it. It is only a bus.)

"Good afternoon, Mr. LeFontaine," she says in her biddy manner (is it only to me she speaks this way?). "We haven't seen you for a while."

"Business has been slow," I say, handing her the thin key. She is dying to know what business, but has never asked. Banks maintain a certain decorum, if you are not asking for money.

She hands me a card to sign, and I sign it below a dozen other of my signatures. She takes the key with a sly smile (is it my white suit? I have a good mind to change banks!) and disappears through the open door of the vault. Through it I can see the neat rectangles of safe-deposit boxes stacked high like drawers at the morgue.

I used to go into the vault with her as a courtesy. Stand beside the small stepladder as she climbed toward the ceiling and opened the double locks and handed down the box. But invariably her flowered dress would pull above her knees as she reached up, revealing a roll of soft white flesh drooping over the tops of the half-stockings she wore. Now I prefer to wait at the desk.

She returns a bit breathless and hands me the metal box (it is large, the kind that frightened authors keep a copy of their manuscripts in). I cradle it under my arm like a football, smile blandly at her, and move to the small rooms in the rear, picking out my usual, second on the left; I set the box and my attaché case on the tabletop attached to the wall. Carefully I

16

lock the opaque glass door behind me.

(It is not the nearest bank. There are several banks in the Quarter. But it is the nearest whose little rooms have opaque doors, and locks.)

I take pleasure in this little room. It is not much bigger than a phone booth, but they keep it neat and clean. The pen always in its place, the blotter, the calendar, the Scotch tape, the scissors chained to the wall. (Curious that all they are afraid of losing is their scissors. One day I will bring a wire cutter in my attaché case and snip the chain and take it. Wipe the smile off her face.)

A shiver of excitement runs through me as I open the metal box and remove the ledger. I set the box on the floor, to make room. (The floor is spotless, too.) I unsnap the attaché case, remove the folder and from it the little clipping. I flip to the back, the anticipation building unstoppably in my chest like when you know you are going to do it and it won't go away until you do. I snip off the correct length of tape and place the top of the clipping exactly along the red line at the top of the ledger; I affix the tape, smoothing it.

Releasing my breath, I allow my eyes to focus on the headline, to see that it is lined up properly. Only that.

NEW DEATH DATE
SET IN SLAYING

I sigh. I suppose we shall never be free of the vulgarisms of journalists. I close the ledger, temporarily.

("How is your mother in Utah?" the mailman said this morning, handing me a three-day backlog of the Salt Lake City *Tribune.* "Just fine," I said, thinking of her in her broken hovel in Philadelphia fifteen years ago. If she is still alive.)

I remove my napkin from the attaché case and spread it on my lap. I take out the silver spoon, the apple, the yogurt, and set them neatly on the tabletop. I remove the top from the yogurt, placing it on the blotter, and spoon some. It has remained as cool as I could hope. (Texture is what matters. The creaminess of the yogurt, the crispness of the apple.)

I savor the taste for a moment. Then I open the ledger and begin from the beginning.

Daralyn Kirk ➤ We rode on his bike like a shooting
horse till the desert fell behind, and green mountains came,
my red dress whipping at my legs. He stopped at a roadside
thing and bought some bags, and under a tree beside a little
river we ate peaches and cherries and grapes. Not like Pinky
with his iron tit under his coat, who ate only meat and cake.
Who left me in Las Vegas for that other.

We rode some more to a big tall park with cliffs crisscrossed
like pink elephant skin reaching up. Zion, it's called, he said,
like his mother's church as a boy. We left the bike and walked
a path to a hanging rock where water dripped all the time.
"Weeping Rock," he read from the sign, and put back his head
like a little nigger boy and catched the drops in his mouth.
And on his face. I sat on the ground tugging my red dress
over my knees and wanted to cry like the rock, alone in the
whole wide world, with Pinky back in Vegas and nothing
ahead but fat ladies on the beach, and maybe them nurses,
too. But I didn't cry. I was afraid he would leave me there.
People is always leaving me places.

He ast if I had any money. I thought of lying but I gave him
from my pocket all the two dollars from the men. We went to
town, and he drug me into a store and held up jeans and shirts
from a rack against me and told me to put them on. I did it
in a little back room and come out with my red dress rolled
up under my arm.

"I think she'll find those more comfortable," the store lady
said.

I looked in the looking glass while he was paying. I couldn't
stop a smile that wet my cheek. Looking back from the glass

18

was one of them cute little college girls, no tits and ass. Except for my high heels. There wasn't no money for shoes.

We rode again and looked at sand all pink like salmon blushing in the afternoon. And took off our shoes and walked through the thicking pink. And rode again, me barefoot, my high heels forgot in all the sand, till we come to another park, the building closed. The ranger looked at his knife and we went to the park. Stone things rose all over, gray and then pink and red, and I couldn't stop myself from laughing on. Them things were great big giant stone men's things, like men when they are ready. Great big stone ones all over, stiffing toward the sky. Toward some great big mouth in the sky. He looked at me stern, as if I shouldn't be laughing.

"Don't you think they're beautiful?" he said.

I nod and say, "They sure is," and can't stop myself from bursting out laughing again. And this time he can't help himself, and he starts laughing too. And puts his arm around my shoulder and walks me back to the bike, and we zoom off to eat in a little place.

It was dark when we come back. He quiets the bike and pulls out blankets from under the seat, and we stretches on the ground under the blankets, soft winds blowing in the trees. I lay still, waiting for him to do it. He doesn't do nothing. He just lays there, his eyes open, staring at the stars. I start to get scared. If you don't do it, people leave you places.

He lays still and I lays still. I think that he is shy and wants me to start. I touch his pants. He takes my hand away.

He lays still and I lays still. Not breathing. My head is dancing with all those giant stone men's things, pink with the sun going down, looming all black in the night. Looming up. I reach over and touch him again. He takes my hand away.

"We can't," he says.

"Why not?" I say, all squirmy.

He didn't say nothing. Then he said, "Your friend Pinky might come back."

"Oh," I said, and then I didn't say nothing. I turned away and went to sleep. Him still looking with eyes like big brown olives at the stars.

Pete Peterson ➤ We were square with the boy. Fair and square. I'm not so sure that he was square with us. The coach lets me watch practice when I want. After all, most of them are my boys. And right from the first day I suspected something. He wasn't moving as quick as he did in the Garden. I figured he was out of shape, he'd come around. I didn't say anything. He certainly looked trim enough in that DeWitt Clinton sweat shirt of his. And he shoots like a dream. Nothing wrong with that.

Before long he's working out with the first team, and then the season comes and he's a starter. He averages fourteen a game and leads the club in assists, and he's the darling of the crowd, with those schoolboy features of his. That even becomes his nickname—Schoolboy Briggs. One game he nets twenty-five. Not bad for a five-eleven guard. And still he's not moving the way he could. I want to say something, but how can you? I figure maybe my eyes are going bad.

Then he goes up for a jumper against Pepperdine and comes down with nobody near him, and his knee buckles under, and he goes down. Just like that. The trainer puts on tape, and he misses two games. He's okay for a while, till the Arizona game. When the exact same thing happens. An eighteen-year-old boy, strong, healthy? That shouldn't happen.

This time the doc takes X-rays and says he needs an operation. Damaged cartilage. He misses the last six games.

He comes to my office in the field house later on. Late-afternoon sun slanting through the windows. Shadows of trackmen running diagonally up the walls as they eclipse the sun outside. He says he'll fly home right after finals—he's holding a B minus—and get the operation and be back on the team next year. But he doesn't have the money, he says. Will the college pay? Since he hurt it playing ball? Well. What do you say to that? Him standing there in beige Levi's, with books under his arm, looking like some ordinary student.

"Your mother has money, right?" I said. "That she was saving for your tuition."

"That's my brother's now," he said, looking me in the eye.

What else could I do? We're not running a charity ward. The doc had warned us that for our caliber of ball he was through. A major gamble at best.

"I'm afraid we'll be needing your scholarship for someone else," I said.

A kid at Verbum Dei. Six-ten.

He stands there, trying to think of what to say. A darkness ripples his face. In his eyes a pained expression I couldn't decipher. Disappointment, I thought then. It was only natural. Finally he turned with no more words and left.

Yeah, I know what they said. If we flew him home he would not have been riding that bike cross-country. And would not have got into this trouble. Well, that's bunkum. If underneath those schoolboy looks the kid is a psycho pervert, which he seems to be, then he's going to do what he did. If not then, then later. Maybe even right on the campus.

The thing that makes my blood boil is those initials. He had no call to drag the school into it. We were always square with him.

Belinda Marshall ➤ When we were through, I
pulled the pale green sheet up under my chin, my bare arms
outside, and smoked, gazing absently at the ceiling. My heart
had not been in it.

"A dime for your thoughts," he said.

"You're hardly keeping up with inflation."

"Okay, a quarter."

I blew a smoke ring. One of these days I am definitely going
to stop. Though I suppose this one after is the one I will miss
the most.

"The same," I said.

"Briggs?"

"Mmm."

"It's done with, Belly. You did all that any lawyer could."

"I wonder sometimes, in the middle of the night. Maybe
someone with more experience . . ."

"There's still the Governor."

"I know. They say he's decent."

"Yeah, but he does have the politics to consider."

"Thanks a lot."

"It's the truth. I don't think you should get your hopes up."

I looked at him sideways and took another puff and blew
smoke at the ceiling.

"It's the only hope we've got."

He took my hand lightly under the sheet.

"You still think he's innocent, don't you?"

For a time I said nothing. Then: "I remember the first time
I saw him. When they brought him to the courtroom for

arraignment. He was shaking like a little lamb."

"A black sheep, no doubt," Eric said.

I pulled my hand away, but let it pass. I didn't feel like fighting. He'd been getting increasingly caustic lately, afterwards. Unless I feigned multiple nirvana.

"He seemed to fade into the wood of the bench as he stood before it. Judge Merton asked him if he had counsel. He didn't know what that meant. 'Do you have a lawyer? Do you have money for a lawyer?' He shook his head. The judge nodded to me—I was sitting in the second row—and I went forward. He said, 'Miss Marshall is an attorney with the Public Defender's office. The court will assign her to represent you in these proceedings until and unless you retain private counsel.' All those big words flying around. All those official faces. He looked lost. I read through the charges and took him aside. 'They say you killed someone.' 'I didn't do it.' 'Then you want to plead not guilty?' He looked into my face, for the first time. Beseeching. His eyes deep and gentle, like a doe's. The crime was brutal, but there was something about him. I believed he was telling the truth."

Eric stroked my belly, under the sheet.

"That was before you knew the evidence."

"So?"

His hand moved lower, searching for dampness. Plunging a finger in, rolling it around. Igniting me with anger. A white flash. It was all a titillating game to him. My work. Walter's life. Why had it taken me two years to realize that?

I pulled away and swung my legs off the bed. I reached for my bikini panties. Size five. If I stop smoking, will I still fit into them? That is something to consider, if it is all over.

"I still believe him," I said. "Despite the jury and the appellate court. And despite you."

"Me? What did I do?"

"Nothing. Listen, I've got to work on that appeal. It's in my head. How about we skip dinner?"

He swung his hairy legs off the other side.

"Yeah, sure. I've got a ton of blue books to mark, anyway. The freshmen are panting for their final grades. 'Using Concrete Examples from the Twentieth Century, Illustrate the Truth of the Adage that Those Who Do Not Study History Are Doomed to Repeat It.' "

"Especially if they fail your course," I said.

He laughed. "Right on. I'm getting to be a mean son of a bitch in my dotage."

I forced a smile and put on a robe. His forty-eight years hung awkwardly in the way he said "right on." Even Walter doesn't say "right on."

I began making notes on a yellow pad as soon as he was out the door.

Leroy Briggs

➤ They asked me if he has a temper. If he ever gets real mad. No, I said, never. He is the calmest person I know.

Sheeet! What they think I was gonna say? He is my brother.

The most time was one night when we were kids. I was eight and he was maybe twelve. The TV was on, we was watching *Daniel Boone*. And then this bulletin come.

"No!" Mama screamed. "No!" And she fell on her knees to the floor and started sobbing and praying, right there on the floor. Me not knowing what was wrong.

Walter didn't say nothing, but stood up from his chair where he was sitting, and stood glaring at the television like he was gonna set it afire with his eyes. And there was nothing on it now but some dumb program again.

"What's the matter, Mama?" I said, but she didn't answer —she was sobbing and moaning and praying all at once. As if the TV was Jesus on the cross. Walter disappeared to his room and came back with his baseball bat.

"Hey, Walter, where you goin'?" I said. He didn't answer but strode toward the door. Mama seen him and called, "You stay here," but he didn't answer. He was already out the door, and me tagging after.

Down the block he walked, banging every house we passed and every fence with his baseball bat. Like to break it. Till he come to the fence by the subway yard. He tossed the bat over, and climbed in after it. Like we always did, to sit on the sloping gravel bed and throw rocks down at the silver tracks below. To see who could hit them the most. Only this time he didn't sit. He picked up the bat and strode down the gravel like walking on a beach, to where a train was parked on a track. It almost dark now with the April sun gone down.

"What you doin', Walter?" I said.

He didn't say nothing, as if I wasn't there, but swung the baseball bat with all his might and smashed in a window on the train.

"Hey, Walter," I said.

He didn't say nothing, but took two steps back and smashed in the next window of the train. Then the next and the next. Down the line he went, smashing with his bat, the glass flying inside the empty train and some of it falling to the gravel at his feet.

"Let me!" I said. "Let me!" Though I couldn't even reach the windows.

He didn't answer. He never took his eyes from that train. Just kept on smashing, his face all grim and set, his eyes burning. Till the bat started splintering. And still he smashed away.

It broke in two when he still had two windows left. Tears was in his eyes now, and he stabbed at the window with the broken piece of handle. Jabbed and jabbed until the window broke. Then he jabbed at the next. And it broke and the handle too. And his hand went through into the train and come out spurting blood across his wrist.

He stepped back from the train, looking at what he had done. Not even noticing it dripping down his pants. Then he saw it and squeezed his wrist with the other hand. And we climbed the fence and went home.

Should I have tole them about that? Sheeet. Blacks was burning down whole entire cities that night, with Martin Luther King shot dead.

The next most time was after they stole the city champs from him. He screamed at the referee till they had to pull him away. Till they hauled and dragged him off to the locker room. He shoved over a bench that was in his way and went to his locker and kicked it. He kicked and kicked, tears washing down his face, till he kicked in the green metal door. Kicked it inside out. I guess you would have to call that a temper, but it's got nothing to do with killing. He's lucky he didn't bust up his own leg.

Harriet Goldberg ➤ We were sleeping in the camper. It was the best vacation we ever had. Herbie had finally stood up to his boss and told him he was taking an extra two weeks. We had four whole weeks to drive through the West. And Wasatch Canyon was the most beautiful of all. Those incredible stone sculptures stretching away as far as the eye could see. As if a thousand Michelangelos had worked to carve them for a thousand years. And all of it done by the wind and the rain. I took two whole rolls of film to show my class. Ektachrome.

I never had them developed.

The sun steaming through the window onto my face woke me early that day. I left Herbie asleep and went outside. The campground was almost empty. So I walked along the path to the john still wearing my nightgown. It wasn't flimsy, no one could see through. When I came out I could see the sun flaming the tops of the rocks. I took a different path, toward the cliffs. The rocks are supposed to be most beautiful right then. Right then at sunrise. Though how they could be more beautiful than at sunset I wouldn't know. They had danced in my brain all night. They wouldn't stop.

I moved toward the cliffs to look. Birds beginning to sing in the trees. But I never got there. Coming around a bend in the path, I saw it. Sticking out of some bushes.

At first I wasn't sure. Maybe it's a mannequin, I thought. Somebody's joke. There are actually people who think practical jokes like that are funny. But it certainly looked like a leg, with some leaves on top.

I was frightened. Who wouldn't be? I took a few steps

closer and peered into the bushes. That's when I screamed. Looking through the bushes and screaming from somewhere deep down inside me. Like I never screamed before. Loud enough to wake the . . . It was horrible. I screamed and screamed and ran like a chicken with its head cut off, looking for the way back to the camper. Till I found it. Herbie pulling his pants on. He sleeps in his Jockey shorts.

"Someone . . . murdered," I gasped, pointing.

"What? Where?"

"We've got to get help. The ranger."

We climbed into the van, and Herbie started driving toward the ranger station. Leaving our cookout equipment and everything. Halfway there we met him in his jeep, coming down. He had heard my screams. We told him to follow us.

At first I couldn't find the place. "Park where we were parked," I told Herbie.

From there I walked toward the john, Herbie and the ranger beside. Then I found the path. "Over there," I said. "Around the bend."

Herbie and the ranger went to look. The campground was scattered with people now, rubbing sleep from their faces. Coming to see what was the matter. Me still in my nightgown.

When Herbie came back to where I was, his face was like a ghost. We hugged each other, tight. As tight as we could.

The things that can happen to people, is all I could think of. The way we take each other for granted.

Simon W. Merton ➤ The crocuses long gone, the forsythia gone, the peonies in full bloom and even beginning to droop a bit, the yellow roses beginning to show their buds. In two weeks there will be yellow roses in front of every house in the neighborhood. A soft peripheral blur, once you leave the courthouse block and the civic grayness of downtown.

I parked the car and walked up the white wooden steps—waiting patiently for me to paint them on the weekend—and smelled something wrong inside. An absence. No smell of soup simmering.

The kitchen was empty; no sandwich on the table, not even a knife and spoon.

"Sarah?"

No answer.

I walked to the foot of the stairs and called up.

"Sarah?"

No answer.

A note, perhaps. An emergency. Then I heard a faint clicking out back. I stepped onto the porch. She was down in the garden on her hands and knees, weeding.

"Sarah?"

Her back was turned. She looked up at me over her shoulder. Then returned to her weeding.

I walked down the steps. Waiting, like the others, for their annual coat of white.

"Don't you know what time it is? It's lunchtime."

She gave no sign that she had heard.

"Did you hear me? Where's my lunch?"

"I'm busy," she said, without looking up. And went on weeding.

"What the . . ."

Then I realized. They must have put it on the radio.

"God damn it, Sarah. I told you, my hands were tied. The law's the law."

She dropped a weed into her basket and began pulling at a larger, tougher one.

"The law can make its own lunch," she said, as if to the stubborn growth.

I started to say something, then stopped. I strode across the lawn and up the bonking stairs, into the kitchen. I threw my suit jacket over the back of a chair, rolled up my sleeves, took a can of Campbell's from the cupboard and began to open it. Halfway around, I stopped. Breathing quickly.

"I won't!" I said aloud, and slammed the can onto the formica.

Tomato soup leaped through the slit and stained my pale blue pants with red spots.

I cursed and went upstairs and changed my suit for a gray.

Women! What is it they see in him? A gentleness, Sarah says. A gentleness covering the death's skull we all carry inside. A chocolate-covered candy. It's unspeakable, what he did. And still they want to mother him. From the first day she sat in on the trial, her mind was made up. She fell in love with him, in her way. That attorney, too. No more than six years older than the boy. Who knows if hers is maternal?

Liberation, they want. If they want liberation they can't keep intuition. One or the other. If they're going to be lawyers and doctors, they've got to deal with facts, not feelings.

I left the house without a word to Sarah out back and drove down Foothill Drive to the Fairview. I sat at the counter and instead of soup ordered a veal cutlet plate with home fries and peas. And a vanilla malt to wash it down. To hell with cholesterol-free.

The one mistake God made in the universe. Giving women the change. She went through the change right around the time of the trial. She hasn't been a fit person to live with since.

I sipped water and swallowed a pill. It was the first time I was eating lunch without her in twenty-three years, except for the time her mother was dying and she went home to Cedar City.

The waitress set down the plate. I took my fork and began to pick at it. I wasn't hungry any more.

Walter Briggs ➤ Death Row is separate. They don't

let us mingle with the other prisoners. Or with each other. We eat by ourselves, and we exercise by ourselves. One hour each day of shooting baskets. And twenty-three hours in the cell.

I asked Jonesy why they keep us alone.

"The official reason," he said, "is so we don't kill the other prisoners. If we did, what could they do to us? We're sentenced to die anyway."

I think, why would we want to kill the other prisoners?

"What's the real reason?" I said.

"The real reason," Jonesy said, "is so the other prisoners don't kill us. Because that would deprive the State of the pleasure."

He has some sense of humor, that Jonesy.

I lie back on my bunk and stare up at the ceiling. It is almost wore out from my staring. The white ceiling is getting darker and darker at the place where I always stare. I swear it.

The thoughts run through my mind again and again, like horses on a merry-go-round. The same horses always winning. The same mistakes. Grinning at me with red-painted lips, like wooden-horse laughs.

If only I hadn't left her. If only I had stayed.

But sometimes a feeling comes over you, and your muscles get all restless in your back and in your legs, and even your bones are ready to leap inside you, and then you got to move. You got to do what you got to do. It happens.

I couldn't sleep that night. I lay there looking up at the stars, and the branches like witches' fingers against the sky. And her beside me. And when I closed my eyes, them rock

33

shapes dancing in my brain, dancing and circling like some wicked Mardi Gras, of this earth and yet not of it. And I thought, I have never before in my life slept outside, under the stars. Always with peeling plaster ceilings above me. Never once before. And I felt I could feel the whole earth turning under me, and the sky above. And her asleep beside. And I thought of school and how I could never go back. The knee would never be the same, and the money was Leroy's now. And how Mama would cry. I guessed maybe I would be a motorman and drive subways in the long winding tunnels under the city, lights picking the tracks out ahead. Thinking about all this with her asleep beside. And then the feeling came, all restless, like I would never sleep again unless I stretched. And I slid out from under the blanket and left her there, and walked quiet up the twisting path to the edge of the cliffs and sat with my legs dangling over, looking at the shapes. The moon was half a moon, with clouds moving by, and the shapes would change their shapes in the moon-dark. When you looked at them, they stayed still. It was only when you closed your eyes that they danced.

A whole hour I must have sat there, thoughts twisting in and among. Till I knew if I didn't sleep it would be a bad day in the morning, and

"Briggs. You got company coming."

It was Jackson, the guard. Standing in the corridor with his dark gray jacket and his badge.

"Company? I ain't expecting nobody."

"Not today," he said. "Later on." And he handed me a postcard through the bars.

"Your mama," he said.

They love to do that. To get you in them little ways.

She could've wrote letters, but it wouldn't matter. They open them anyway.

"Briggs's mama is coming all the way from New York to kiss him good-bye," he calls out to Jonesy. And laughs that laugh of his and moves on.

I lay down on the bunk and read the postcard. Her usual big writing with a blue ball-point pen that skips.

Dear Son,

How are you? I went to see the Reverend and he is no help atall. I cant sit here and watch the days go by and do nothing before [before was crossed out, but I could still read it]. So I am coming on the bus to see you next week. And to see that guvornor and beg [beg was crossed out, too] and ask him for clemensy. Somewhere out there is a murderer who might confess and you will be free and clear. They got to do nothing to you till then. Don't lose faith I will see to it. Your loving

Mama

I read the card again, and then I folded it in half and stuck it in my pocket. And stared up at the ceiling, at the dark spot I was wearing out. It would be better if she didn't come. It will only make it worse.

After a time Jonesy calls out, "That true?"

"What?"

"That your mother's comin' out."

"Yeah," I said. Feeling like a first-class turd.

Jonesy shakes his head. I can't see him, but I know he is shaking his head, like he always does.

"It's like I always say," he says. "If you got to kill someone, you start with your family first. It makes it easier all around."

He has some sense of humor, that Jonesy. Only sometimes I think he ain't kidding.

Estelle Hawthorne ➤ I worked it with him like I do

each year. Called the college employment for some strong young man to move furniture and boxes. It's always athletes they send. Strong young jocks on scholarship who need extra spending money. If I don't like them, I call again a few days later, for another. Him I kind of liked from the beginning.

He had on a college T-shirt and red basketball shorts that must have been from high school. Just a freshman, he was. I had him move some things in the garage. Work up a sweat.

"Take off your shirt," I said. "It doesn't smell like roses."

He pulled it off, sheepish. It's not hard to cow them. His lean brown body moist and glistening.

"I need some boxes down from the top of a closet," I said. And took him up to the bedroom and put the rickety chair beside. "You can stand on that."

He climbed up and got hold of a box. I was wearing my yellow shorts and too-big yellow halter, and from up there he couldn't help looking in.

"Don't fall," I said, and moved to steady him. My arm around his buttocks, my cheek against his pants.

He got the box down, with relief.

"That other one too," I said. "The one in the back."

He climbed back up on the chair, awkwardly this time, his pants stretched tight. And reached back.

"I'll help you," I said. And put my arm gently around him. Him straining to reach the heavy box in the back. Straining all over.

And then me unzipping him, slowly, with the other. Pulling it out. Letting it breathe.

I would've done it that way, but I was afraid he'd go weak and fall and maybe hurt himself. Instead I took his hand.

"Come down," I said.

There was nothing he could do but obey. Climb down from the rickety chair, sticking straight out like a flagpole.

"Lie down," I said, leading him.

He hesitated. As if he were afraid to put his sneakers on the bed.

"I'll be late for practice."

Then he did as I said.

Forrest Stone ► Wild woman's screams came floating in on the dawn. I thought I was dreaming. Then I had to piss real bad and knew I was awake. And still hearing the screams. Like a hog with its throat half cut.

I threw on my uniform and hopped into the jeep and went racing down toward the campground. Halfway there a van was coming up, a man driving, a woman hysterical beside.

"Help! Murder!" she starts screaming, like in the movies.

"Follow me," the man says, calm at least.

We ride down and she can't find the place, and I'm thinking it was *her* bad dream. Murder, here in the park? Twisted ankles we get, mostly. A broken leg, once. Once in ten years.

"Over there," she says.

I walk around the path on the familiar red earth, and then I see it. And peer into the bushes and get half sick to my stomach. And stand there cursing at nobody. Cursing at whoever did it.

People start coming around then, wakened by the lady's screams, following the jeep noise to the place.

"Keep back," I say. "Go on about your business. There's nothing you want to see here."

Like fun. They all want to see. Pressing around for a look. Some of them forgetting they got their own kids trailing behind.

"Get those kids out of here!" I scream.

I leave the man standing guard—he doesn't look too good —and run down to the jeep and get a rope. And tie it on the bushes around. Roping off the crime scene.

I ask the man how he's doing. "Okay," he says. I scoot back

to the jeep and call Jenkins at the State Police. He's home sleeping, but his new deputy is on. Scott, I think.

"You better wake Jenkins," I tell him. "We got us a pretty bloody corpse up here. Down at the campground."

I walk back up and stand near the rope, the people buzzing like flies. Till then I had not given a thought to who did it. It could've been anybody. Some people stop at the Visitors' Center before they come on out to see. But I don't pay them no mind, unless they ask a question. Others drive straight on in without stopping, and see the park and drive out. Others drive right in and camp. Charlie Manson could've been in that campground last night and nobody would've known. Who dunnit isn't my job.

Then she came wandering up, like in a daze. She peered into all the faces, and then she came straight to me. I guess because of the uniform.

"Where is he?" she said.

"Where is who?"

"He. Him."

Then I remembered. Those bruises.

"What do you mean?" I said. "Isn't he with you?"

"No. He done gone and left me. Why did he have to leave me?"

"When did he leave?" I said.

"In the dark. He couldn't sleep and wandered off to them cliff. And come back and I was scared. Don't be scared, he said. And touched my hair. And lay down beside me. And then I heard yelling, and the sun. And he was gone. And his bike gone too."

"What time was that?" I said.

She shook her head.

"Why did he have to leave me?" she said. "I was willing to do it."

It was no real evidence, of course. A guy ditching a broad. She was no grade-A catch in the brains department, if you know what I mean. Standing there just mumbling.

Then I almost smacked myself on the forehead. I don't know where my own brains were at. 'Cause that's just about the blade it would have took. Something at least that big. I scooted to the jeep and called again, to get his description out before he got too far. But they weren't there. They must have left already.

I went back to the crime scene to wait. Those people hanging around like it was the high point of their holiday. Some of them with cameras now, snapping the leg sticking out.

Josephine Briggs ➤ Who could've thought they

would be so angry. As if they would die from dirty house while I was gone. And them too lily-pure to lift a rag.

"But, Josephine, I'm having forty people over on the thirtieth for little Stevie's junior high graduation . . ."

"But, Josephine, we've got to do all the furniture and put on the slipcovers for the summer. This is all so sudden . . ."

"We'll be taking our own vacation in August, Josephine. Couldn't you take yours then too? That way you wouldn't lose any . . ."

My sick old mama needs me now, down in Georgia, I tole them. I'll be gone two weeks or so. (May she rest in peace, like they say.)

I went to the bank and took out Walter's—Leroy's—college money. Half I put in my purse. The other I divided in two and put half inside my brassiere and half inside my stocking, inside my shoe. I put on my black dress for fune . . . for church-going, and packed a suitcase I borrowed from Cora, and told Leroy to eat his suppers there and mind his manners and make sure he locked the door when he went out. And I waited till late after dark, so no one would see me leaving with a suitcase, 'cause otherwise they break right in, sure as gold. And I took the Dyre Avenue all the way down to 42nd Street. To the Port Authority. They tole me to take a bus to Chicago, and from there I get a bus to Utah.

I wait in the station an hour, with drunks sleepin' on the floors, and cops come chasing 'em, and the drunks keep coming back. Then the bus come, and I give the driver my ticket, and he tried to take my suitcase for underneath. But I

41

wouldn't let him. I took it on the bus and put it on the rack overhead, where I could see it. And took a seat by the window, looking out.

The bus stood there a long time, waiting to fill up. I took out a tissue in the half-dark and wiped my eyes. The bus kept reminding me of that other bus. We was going up to the mountains, for a week in the country. "The boys got to see what the country's like," Harold said, and he arranged the whole thing. We took the bus and waiting up in Liberty there would be a cabin rented for a whole week, right on a lake, where the boys could run and swim. Halfway the bus stopped at Ellenville, and Harold took the boys off to buy them candy. And the boys come back eating Snickers and say Harold will be along in a minute. We wait and wait, and no Harold. I go out and look all around. Then the bus driver say he can't wait no more, we got to get off or get on. There was no place to stay there, so we got on and went to Liberty, where sure enough the cabin was waiting. And the boys played and swimmed all week, happy as clams. And no word from Harold, till the postcard come at home two weeks later. And ten postcards since. One every year, at Christmas.

"Going to Chicago?" the fat lady said.

She was so fat her hips was pressing into mine, and those seats were plenty wide.

"Huh," I said.

"Chicago," she said. "Going to Chicago?"

"Utah," I said.

"My, that is far," she said. "I'm going to Chicago. To see my second grandson. My Ruthie just had a little boy."

She opened a fat bag on her lap and pulled out one of them cellophane folders of pictures.

"That's the older one, Greg," she said. "Course I don't have a picture of Michael. He was just born Friday. And there's my Ruthie, of course, and that's her Harold."

I inhale my breath and take the pictures from her. He is a nice-looking young man.

"You going to visit your daughter?" she says.

"My son," I say. Caught abrupt. I give the pictures back.

"That's nice. What does he do in Utah?"

"College. He's in college there."

"My, my, that is nice. Isn't college over, though, it bein' the middle of June?"

I wished she would go away. Just disappear and leave me be. But she would be there all to Chicago.

"Summer school," I say.

"Oh," she say. "Well, I guess for some it's rougher than others. You take my Ruthie's Harold. He went to Harvard on one of those scholarships, you know, and he just breezed right through. And on to Harvard law school he went. The times they are achangin', aren't they?"

The bus coughed up and started. I looked out the window, at yellow lights running like rain down the tile walls of the terminal. And on through tunnels out into darker night.

Lloyd Jenkins ➤ We took dozens of pictures, from

every angle. We looked for footprints, but it was hopeless, all those people milling around, thousands of tourist sneaker prints in the red clay. It's gonna be a bitch, I thought as soon as I saw the body. If I don't find him quick, there'll be a stink all the way to the Governor's office. What with the tourist season just beginning.

When we had enough, we hauled the body out of the bushes and down onto a stretcher, and took more pictures, full view. That's when the first break came. The blood was drying on the chest in the morning sun, and I saw it was all uneven. Dark cuts deeper than the rest, but with a pattern. I knelt down to look. And damned if there weren't two initials carved into that poor guy's chest. Two initials with periods after, a good two inches high, maybe more. The son of a bitch had signed his work of art.

Flies were buzzing around, so I covered the body with a sheet. We put it in the back of the ambulance, and I spread the men out, combing the bushes and the campground. For clothing, signs of struggle, some identification of the victim. Also the murder weapon. If he left it behind.

The ranger—Stone, I think it was—was busy keeping the curious away. I called him over and asked him more about this black boy he told me about. What with the blade he had and skipping out in the night, he certainly seemed like a person I would want to talk to. About events.

"You know his name?" I said.

"No."

He looked around, at the people milling there like they had nothing better to do. Then he pointed to a girl, off by herself, leaning against a tree about a hundred yards away. Not exactly leaning against it, but sort of hugging it around with her arms. Her cheek against it. As if for consolation.

"That's the one he was with," he said. "With the beat-up face. I guess she would know his name."

I climbed the sloping ground to the girl. She didn't change her position. Hugging that tree for dear life. She was older than I expected, but dressed like a kid. And barefoot. Purple welts under her eyes, like he said.

"I'm Lieutenant Jenkins," I said. "State Police. I'd like to ask you a few questions."

She heard me but didn't look at me. Her eyes were far away, past the trees, out over the canyon.

"Who is the man who beat you up?" I said.

"I dunno," she said. Just like that.

"How can it be that you don't know?"

She kept on hearing without looking.

"I dunno," she said again.

I was beginning to get a little angry. She was my first real witness. I took her chin, gently, and turned it to make her look at me. Then I eased off. She seemed to be in some kind of daze.

"Relax," I said. "No one is going to hurt you." I tried to look sympathetic. "What's your name?"

"Daralyn," she said, looking over my shoulder at the far-off clouds.

"Daralyn what?"

"Daralyn Kirk Twenty-two Edgemere Miami." As if it were one word.

"Okay, Daralyn," I said softly. "What was the name . . ."

"Why did he have to leave me?" she said. "I was willing to do it."

"Who?"

"He. Him."

"The boy on the bike?"

She looked at me then for the first time, with a kind of desperation.

"You know where he is?" she said.

"Not yet. But I'll help you find him. If you can tell me his name. I need his name to find him."

Her eyes squinted, as if she was trying to decide if she could trust me. Then she started thinking, real hard. So's you could see what she was doing. I waited and waited.

Finally she said, "Honda."

"Honda? He told you his name was Honda?"

"Weren't no need to ask him," she said. "It was writ there on his bike."

I couldn't decide whether to laugh or get mad. There's nobody in three counties that stupid.

I looked down at the ground, grinding the red clay with my shoe. Then I looked at her face, her pale eyes almost more albino than blue. As if the intelligence had been washed right out of them. A maniac running loose, and this is what I had. And the day getting awfully warm for May.

"Come with me," I said. And took her hand and led her down, toward where the ravens were circling high above. She hopping and wincing over the earth, as if she was not used to walking barefoot. With her toenails polished a bright red, but chipped. And me having misgivings about doing it. But there was the Governor to think about. And this guy could kill again before dark.

When we reached the ambulance, the sun glinting off it blindingly, she shaded her eyes with her hands.

"Why'd he have to leave me?" she said. "I was willing to do it."

I pulled open the back doors, the handles hot as a bitch. The sheet looking cool inside.

"Pull off the sheet," I said.

"What for?"

I was beginning to get frustrated.

"Pull it off!" I said. And shoved her toward it.

She stumbled forward and caught herself. She looked at me and then past me, where the others had gathered around. And then at the dim inside, and grabbed hold of the bottom of the sheet with her left hand and began pulling it toward herself, slowly. Till it dropped in a heap at her feet.

She stood there, looking at that poor wretch inside. Saying nothing. No screams. No nothing.

Finally she turned to look at me. Her face even more dazed than before. She still hadn't made a sound. But tears were moving down her cheeks. Making the purple welts glisten.

"Get him out of here," I said to Scottie. And I took her hand and led her away, into some cool shade, and sat her on a log. A nuthatch singing overhead.

"Okay, Daralyn," I said, gentle as could be. "You and me are gonna have a talk."

Walter Briggs ➤ I lay on my bunk and stare at the dark spot on the ceiling that is getting always darker as I stare. I whisper to myself if I am afraid to die. My voice whispers back no. But my heart starts running and the sweat breaks out, and in my skin and bones the answer is always yes. For no reason.

It's like that cat in the yard. There is an alley cat that lives in the exercise yard. The guards must feed him, I guess. Every day when I go out to shoot baskets he is there in the yard, waiting. I don't like cats—I never did—staring out of under parked cars with shiny eyes. Evil eyes. When I have nightmares it is usually of cats creeping up on me. Always has. I don't know why. Maybe some clawing cat jumped on my face as a baby in the crib. Or maybe they remind me of rats.

Whatever reason, I don't like that cat hanging around trying to rub on my leg. It makes me sweat all over. So when I start shooting baskets after the guard leaves, I make sure a rebound bounces hard toward the cat, and me running after. And the cat leaps up to the top of the wall and watches from there till I am done.

The cat is gray, with green eyes. It is medium size. I ask myself why I am afraid of it. For that is the only true word, though I would never let on. It is silly to be afraid, because there is nothing it could do to me. If I stamp my foot, it runs, and I could kill it with a kick if I wanted. And it can't even really bite me, like a dog. So there is no reason to be afraid. And still I am.

It is the same with dying. I look at the whole world. Every person that was ever born has died. In the whole of history.

48

Old people weak with no brains left, they die. Strong people in the midst of life, they crash their car and die. Even little babies get sick and die. Without being afraid. All animals die. Even fruits and vegetables. Every thing that ever has life, it is going to die. From the minute we are born there is no doubt we is going to die. Millions and billions of people have died, every last one. So why should me, of all of them, be afraid? Afraid to do what all of them have done? What must be done?

All the same, I am afraid.

Jonesy ain't. "Nine more days," he sings out this morning. Like it's a joke. Meaning he gets it in nine more days. And he ain't afraid.

With me it's different, of course. I am not going to die, now. Not here. Maybe in a bed when I am old and gray, and then I will not be afraid. I hope. But not this. This is like some high walled puzzle from which there will soon be a way out. They will see it is all a mistake, and they will unlock the gates, and I will go out again into the world, with still time to make Mama proud. And some sweet young thing still growing up for me. And all possibilities.

I know that is the truth.

Belinda Marshall ► Eric stayed over again. It wasn't good.

It should have ended weeks ago. Neither of us had the nerve.

We finally exploded this morning. It was ugly. I guess you shouldn't let things slide.

I didn't make breakfast, just coffee. I wanted him out, quick. And he was in no mood to stay.

"I don't have much time," I said, pouring. "I'm driving out to see Walter."

"Walter who?" he said. Just to irritate.

"My client."

I picked up my coffee. It was too hot. I put it down.

"What for?" he said, sipping his. Me thinking, I hope he burns his tongue.

"I'm writing that appeal to the Governor. I want to go over everything with him one more time. Maybe he'll remember something that didn't come out at the trial."

"A sudden, illuminating fact that will prove his innocence, for all to see?"

He was mocking me.

"Something like that," I said.

Eric sipped again and put down his cup.

"Do you realize what you're doing, Belly? He's not just your client any more. You're not going out there for evidence. Why not admit it? You just want to see him one more time. See that warm chocolate flesh again before it turns cold. Like his mother, or a wife. You're too involved. You've been diddling this case for two years. It will ruin your career if you don't move on to other things."

I looked at him across the table, stonily. He was dabbing his precious brown-turning-gray goatee with his napkin. I was beginning to despise his every mannerism.

"You still hate him, don't you?" I said.

"You don't hate a gnat that buzzes around your head. You just swat it, and it's done."

I wished I was dressed. I wished I was wearing something more than a robe. The one that he had given me.

"Is that so?" I said. "And they can't swat him soon enough for you, can they? Jesus, Eric, I don't believe your attitude. He's an innocent boy, and they're going to kill him. And to you he's just a bug. What if he were different? What if he were a militant black radical? A George Jackson or a Bobby Seale? Screaming for the blood of all white men. For the rape of all white women. That would be different, wouldn't it? That would give you a nice delicious tingle. It would fit in with your historic theories of oppression. You know what you would be doing then? You'd be picketing outside the prison. 'Free Walter Briggs.' You'd be signing petitions for the ACLU. You'd even draft a protest for the AAUP. Start a legal defense fund. Hire Bill Kunstler to defend him. And never mind if he was guilty as sin. Even murder would be justified by the lilt of his rhetoric. But now? He happens to be a nice kid who somehow didn't learn to hate. Maybe his great-grandfather was a slave —I don't know. But his mother worked hard to bring him up straight, and his father too, for a while. And he went to school and played basketball and got himself a scholarship so he could go to college. He's trying to make it in the white man's world instead of fighting it. Is that a crime? It happens to be the only real world around."

"His crime is murder one," Eric said coolly. "It's time you faced the facts and dropped the innocent shit."

My cigarette had gone out during my harangue. I tried to light another and had trouble striking the match. Finally I got it lit.

"You, the big civil libertarian," I said. "Always looking for the racial angle. Has it ever occurred to you that if he was white he would have gotten twenty years to life, at most? Or that he might not even have been convicted on circumstantial evidence? Or has your personal involvement blinded your concern for justice?"

"Me?" he said. "*My* involvement? Don't make me laugh. You know, Belfy, ever since he lost his appeal you've been a dead fish. As if you've been sleeping with a dead man. And you know why? Because you have been sleeping with a dead man. With him! Only he's locked away in that cell, and I'm the nearest you could come. Probably you would have preferred his basketball coach. He was a lot closer, used to see him naked in the locker room. But Barstow is fat and sweaty, and a good Catholic with eight kids and the fear of God in him. So you turned to me instead. A substitute nigger."

My hands were shaking. My whole body was shaking.

"Get out," I said.

He stood, abruptly. His chair fell over backward, clattering.

"You're damn right I'll get out," he said. "I'm tired of being surrogate penis for your black bastard murderer."

He walked from the table, not to the door but the other way, toward the bathroom. When he came back he had something in his hand.

"Here," he said. "Think of me when you're diddling yourself with this. I hope you're happy together."

And snapped his purple toothbrush in half and tossed both pieces onto the table.

I stood and looked around, wildly, for some object. Any object. *Newsweek* had come in the mail and was on the table. I grabbed it and threw it at his face. It struck him in the chest and flapped, harmlessly, to the floor.

"Have a nice life," he said.

And walked to the door and was gone.

I sat down again, shaking even more than before. I wanted to throw up. Instead I stared into my still-hot coffee. It was there, I had known it was there, and couldn't pretend that I hadn't. And had reached past it for the magazine instead.

No guts, Belinda. In times of crisis no guts. And you want to be a lawyer?

Leroy Briggs ➤ Cora babbles on too much, so I leave right after dinner. "Got homework to do," I say. The sacred word. And come home to the apartment, triple-empty now with Mama gone on that bus ride to goosechase. The only light in the black room from the rolling television, still on like I left it. The vertical knob broken, a thick black bar cutting the screen across. Cutting off heads. Like they used to do to kings, in the olden days.

Leroy means king, in French. *Le roi.* That's what he told me once. Saw it in one of Pa's old books from N'Yorleans.

I try not to think of him. I keep on thinking of him. That time at Lake Jonah in the mountains. The first lake I ever saw, and Walter too. We put on our new red bathing suits and went running down through the grass that tickled my feet. The water hit my toes like cubes of ice, and I stopped. Walter ran right in and dove at the water and disappeared under as if he already drowned, and came up kicking and splashing. He never swam in his life before, but he kicked and splashed his arms till he reached that pretty white raft sitting out in the middle.

I stood on the wet grass looking out at him. Then I did what I always did with Walter. I copied. I ran into the water and dove on my flat-out belly. And went under with my mouth open, breathing water and swallowing water and coming up choking and going down again. Like I would drown. And Walter splashing back in from the raft to save me. But Mama, who'd been sitting on her lawn chair on the grass, got there first, in her socks and shoes and all, and pulled me out. I wasn't in very far.

"That's enough for the first day," Mama said to me when I stopped choking, sitting on the grass.

"He's got to go back in," Walter said, "or he'll always be afraid."

"Time enough tomorrow," Mama said.

"I'll stay with him," Walter said. "I'll hold his hand."

Mama was right. I didn't wanna go. Not just yet. But it was always the same with Walter. I followed.

We walked in slowly this time, till the water was at our waists. Him holding my hand. Me shaking.

"Just put your head under like this," he said. "With your mouth closed and not breathing." And he ducked his head and showed me.

I was scared, but I tried it, him still holding my hand. It wasn't as hard as it looked. Same thing with holding on to him and kicking my feet. And after that splashing with my hands. It wasn't half an hour before I swam out to that raft, Walter swimming beside me. He had this way of making you feel you was safe. My chest bursting and proud as we sat on the white raft together, feet dangling in the water, looking in toward shore. Toward Mama, sitting on the yellow lawn chair like a sailor's widow looking out to sea. Though probably I didn't think that then. I was too happy then and didn't even know that he was gone.

Pa then, now Walter. My mind comes back. I get up and go to my room. Next to Walter's, whose door we keep closed.

And get all angry again. Thinkin' of what to do.

Lloyd Jenkins ➤ Getting that woman-child to talk was like pulling teeth. I say woman-child advisedly, because she could have been either. I asked her how old she was. When she was born. She said she didn't know. You could tell she was telling the truth.

From her face, she could have been thirty-five. Lines around the eyes, a tight, drawn look. Like a good looker beginning to be used up. But she was dressed like a kid, in blue jeans and a western shirt. From ten feet away you would have guessed she was twenty at most. Which couldn't be. But when she sat down on that log she jiggled good and firm underneath. Not yet droopy at all. Twenty-six, I'd say, within a year or two.

I began to ask her questions. Review the pertinent events of the night before. Like pulling teeth, as I said. She seemed to drift off into her own world at times. A world swarming with pronouns. He. Him. Them. She wasn't too good with names.

Halfway through, Scottie came over, carrying a clean white towel suspended across both hands. A knife lying lengthwise, like a corpse. With smears of dried blood.

"We found it on a ledge, below the cliff," he said. "He must have thought he was throwing it into the canyon. And didn't see the ledge in the dark. It was lying in plain view, gleaming in the sun."

I had him show it to the girl.

"You ever see that before?" I said.

She looked at it, and through it, in that dazed way of hers. Finally she said, "It was his'n," in her voice from far away.

I looked up at Scottie. He nodded.

"The ranger says that's the one," he said. "Says there probably aren't two knives like that in the whole state of Utah. Let alone in this park last night."

I pursed my lips and wiped my hand across.

"Any I.D. on the victim yet?" I said.

Scottie shook his head.

"Okay," I said. "Put out an A.P.B. on that boy. Wanted for suspicion of murder."

I looked at the woman-child. She was looking at her bare feet. As if fretting that her bright red toe polish was chipped. I don't think she knew what was going on. Too dumb to know how lucky she was. That she could have been the one under that sheet.

Walter Briggs ➤ The toilet is right there against the
wall, in the middle of the cell. No door, no stall, no nothing.
You got to sit there in plain view. Sometimes I think that's the
worst. The most dehuman. Izing. What do they think I would
do if there was a door?

I sit, thinking again of that shot. An obsession, it's becoming. If only I hadn't thought those thoughts, right before the
shot. Those stupid thoughts. Superstition is all it was. Like
when I was a kid, listening to the Mets. Thinking, if I don't
uncross my legs, Cleon will hit a homer. How dumb can you
get? There I was, stealing the ball with four seconds left,
breaking down court, going up for the jumper—and thinking
that stupid thought. And going crazy mad when the ref said
it don't count.

And look what's happened since. It makes you believe superstition is true after all.

"Hey, Briggs."

It's Jonesy, calling out.

"What?"

"How come you never get mad?"

"Mad at what?"

"You know. Everything. Being here. You say you didn't do
it. Doesn't it make you mad?"

"Sure it makes me mad."

"How come you never show it, then?"

Sometimes I have nice dreams. Of when I was a kid, and Pa
and us all together. A Fourth of July picnic, with hot dogs and
soda, and three-legged races, and everything. And I'm hopping toward the finish line with one leg in a sack, and some

57

cute little girl I don't even know my partner. And we're gonna win it together. And just before we win I wake up, looking at the ceiling. At first I don't remember where I am. Then I see the bars, and I remember. And I get so depressed and mad I want to die. I lay there on the bunk till the feeling passes.

"What good would it do to get mad?" I say. "There's bars and walls and guards with guns. There's nothing I can do but wait. If I let myself get mad I'd go crazy."

"You're wrong, kid," Jonesy says. "It's if you don't let it out. That's when you go crazy."

I finish and wipe myself and pull up my pants. We don't wear stripes, like in prison movies. Blue denims, we wear.

"You get mad?" I say.

"You kidding?" Jonesy says. "Don't you hear my mouth?"

"Yeah. I guess."

"Besides," he says, "with me it's different."

"Why is that?"

I hear him striking a match on the wall. Lighting a cigarette.

"Because they got me fair and square," he says.

I don't say nothing. That one needs time to sink in. I never heard him say that before.

"What do you mean?" I say. Just loud enough so he can hear.

He's puffing on his cigarette, blowing smoke. I can see it drifting in the corridor, in and among the bars. Unbound.

"Life's a game," he says. "Like chess. There's rules. Early on, I made a rule for myself. I would do whatever I wanted. Not spend my life in some factory for the rich bastards. But you need money to live, right? So I take it. As long as I'm smart enough not to get caught, I win. If I get caught—well, there's rules for that, too. They take you off the board."

"And you got caught?" I say. Dumbly.

"Three times," he said. "First two was only check."

He puffed again and blew smoke through the bars.

"Third time this old man in the diner pulled a gun from underneath. Damn fool. I had to shoot. It was self-defense. The law don't see it that way, of course, but that's what it was, at that moment."

I didn't say anything.

"I couldn't leave those witnesses, of course."

"They caught you anyway," I said. Sympathetic-sounding.

"Checkmate," he said. "Over and out. But you get my point?"

"Yeah," I said. Not certain.

"My point is, *I* got no reason to be mad. And I'm mad anyway. But *you*—you got all the reason in the world to be mad. It's only human. And you'd better let it out, boy, or it'll drive you crazy."

"Yeah," I say. And stretch out on my bunk. And try to forget what he said. And keep my eyes away from the darkening spot.

Josephine Briggs ➤ The fat lady fell asleep right away. I thank the Lord for that. Breathing like a twelve-year dog on a summer-dust Georgia road. Her hips heaving against me and rolling off with the tidal rhythm of seas and fat black mamas.

Myself, I don't need much sleep any more. Haven't for two years now. No earth mama cleaning white folks' houses. "More like a scarecrow," Cora says. I tell her she's just jealous. Her having to diet all the time.

Outside the window flat black night rolling by. Jersey Turnpike, Pennsylvania, one of them. Not even street lights, just the bus eyes shining like a bug.

Instead of Walter, I find myself thinking of Leroy left at home. Which is odd. It hits me like a jolt. I don't think I have really thought about Leroy in two years. He is just there, around the house. To be told what to do. His face taken on a heaviness, a lumpiness, ever since his brother went away. Growing to manhood under my eyes, while my eyes weren't looking.

I can't help myself, with him locked up out there, like a caged bird. He was always the graceful one. The love child. Leroy the marriage child. Plodding after like the wooden cart after the dancing horse. It's supposed to be the other way, they say. The younger one the more poetic. Not with them. It's Walter who always set one eye off on the stars. Like his father before him. A motorman he wanted to be as a child, driving trains through shiny tracks in the darkness. The idea calling to something in his brain, like train whistles in the night. Till the chance for college come from that part of him that's better than he knows. While Leroy pumps gas on weekends at the station and acts content.

"You want to be a mechanic, learn to fix the engines?" Mr. Hemus said to him one day.

"What for?" Leroy said. And went on pumpin' gas.

Won't be no need for his college money for college.

The bus curves onto a ramp, changing one highway for the next. Thin edges of water streaking the windows in dots. A light rain while everyone sleeps. All except me and the driver, moving on.

I shame to remember my thoughts so many times, late at night. About the two of them. So shameful I never tole them to anyone. Thoughts not for that dumb Reverend's ears. How can you help your thoughts, even if you know they be wrong? That that one be here. And this one be there instead. A thought no mother should have.

It would never be, of course. Walter stop for that girl out of politeness. And left her out of the same. To try to be kind. Leroy might never have stopped. And if he did, he would not have left her be. I say that even if he's my son. I hear him with Angel already, at sixteen. It's nature's way.

I love them both. And they each other. It just seems like all the grace we had was pumped into that first one, and not enough left over for the second. It's my fault and Harold's, not theirs.

I remember one time Leroy asked him why Harold had gone away. Why their pa had left them. Walter turned it into a fairy tale, right there in the kitchen, over franks and beans.

"Once upon a time there was the King of the Horns," he said. "The King of the Horns made the prettiest music in the whole wide world, 'cause there was music in his soul. He had a golden trumpet, and when he blew it people came from all over, down to the Southland, to hear his music, and have peace restored to their souls.

"One day the King of the Horns met a beautiful dark-skin lady. She was tall and thin and had bright flashing eyes. And the King of the Horns fell in love with the dark-skin lady. And he married her and made her his Queen. And together they moved to the Northland, where the dark-skin lady had her sisters and brothers and where she lived.

"Soon a Prince was born to them. The Prince of Horns. And then another, the Baby Brother of Horns. Only they didn't call them that. 'Cause by then the horn was packed away in a closet. It was cold in the Northland, and pretty music froze. So the King of the Horns had put away his trumpet and his purple robes, and he spent his days shampooin' rugs.

"Ten years passed, and the Royal Family lived like any other family in the Northland. But all the time the King of the Horns was shampooin' rugs, the music was backing up in his heart. Till one day it was near to bursting. So he packed up the Queen and the little Princes, and he took them to a pretty lake far away in the mountains, where they would be safe and happy. And then he took down his golden horn and shined it up, and he went off by himself, traveling to the Southland and all over. Making music again. Restoring peace to them that came to listen."

He finished talking, just like that. Leroy, listening, shoved more beans in his mouth and chewed and swallowed and said, "When you comin' to the part about Pa leavin'?"

Walter looked at me with a helpless look on his face. As if to say, "What we gonna do with this chile?"

All the time me thinking, how'd you dare dream up such jive malarkey as that?

And wanting to smack him for it.

And wanting to hug him for it, too.

Estelle Hawthorne ➤ If it wasn't so tragic I think

I'd laugh. Pseudo-tragic, as my husband would say, lacking heroic stature. But it sure was funny at the beginning. All those myths about black boys and their prowess. Manchild in the Promised Land. Screwing their cousins on the roofs of tenements when they are nine.

Maybe some of them do. But Walter? When he came to me, Walter had a cherry as big as a watermelon.

So to speak.

Why'd he keep coming back, then?

Why else? It was the best damn course he took in college. A complete education. Three hours a week, no credits. With Edward and Jill off in Berkeley looking on from their photographs beside the bed in high-school caps and gowns. Watching their mother do it.

"Poor Estelle," I imagine the neighbors whispering. "The professor's wife has got her generation gap between her legs."

As if everyone doesn't!

He used to shake sometimes, all brown over my slightly sagging whiteness. And other times throw quick little glances over his shoulder. He never got over the fear that any minute the bedroom door would open and Eric would walk in.

As if Eric would have given a damn.

Daralyn Kirk ➤ He took me to that ambulance and made me pull off the sheet. I didn't want to do it, but he made me. And underneath a person all covered with blood. Like them.

They shouldn't oughta left me. Me in the back seat eating a chocolate ice cream cone. My favorite. And holding a big brown teddy bear Papa won me at the fair. And them talking and yelling at each other, and I hit my head, and there is chocolate ice cream all over my face and the teddy bear I fell on. And the car not moving any more. And both windows broken and them with blood on their face. Blood all over them slumped together in the front seat and not saying nothing. And sirens and lights in my eyes. And they looking at my head and took me to the hospital. And then to that place where all the children were. Them laughing at me 'cause my teddy bear has chocolate ice cream all over. And then to that place with the nurses. And they never come to see me. They left me through them broken windows and never come back. Not ever. They shouldn't oughta left me. And tears on my cheeks 'cause that man in the sheet done gone away like them. Whoever.

He sit me on a log, and he ask me about He. Him. I told him about the bike and the ride and them cherries and them clothes. And how when we lie together under that blanket I touched his pants, and he took my hand away. And I touched him again, and he said we can't. I don't know why he left me. I was willing to do it. He asked me about that again. I told him again, and he wrote things in a book.

Go on, he said, and I told him I went to sleep with him still looking at the stars. And then I woke up hearing creakies in the bush, and he is no longer beside me. And I look around and he is gone. And I am frightened to be alone. And then he come back and lie down beside me. And told me not to be scared. And I told him of the noise, and he said it was him walking. And there was nothing to be ascared of. And he hold my head on his chest, and I fall asleep. And I wake up hearing screaming and the sun. And he is gone, and his bike gone too. He shouldn't oughta left me.

Why did he leave you? he said. I dunno, I said. Because he did that to that man? he said. What man? I said. That man in the ambulance, he said. No, I said. He was nice. He wouldn't do no thing like that.

Then this other man came holding a knife. It was his all right. With dry blood all over. Like chocolate.

Let's go back, he said. When he was walking around in the night, what was he doing? Was he doing that to that man? I dunno, I said. Then why did he tell you not to be afraid? he said. 'Cause I was afraid, I said. Why were you afraid? he said. You were afraid he would do it to you too, right? So he told you not to be afraid, that he wouldn't do it to you. He told you what he did to that man, right? Or maybe he took you and showed you, right? And then he said don't be afraid, he wouldn't do it to you.

No, I said. He wouldn't do something like that.

He look around. Some bird was singing in the trees.

That was his knife, wasn't it? he said. It looked like it was, I said. Then he must have done it to that man, he said. I dunno, I said.

He look at the ground and rub his shoes in it. Me, I had no shoes. Just barefoot with my nail polish chipped. Pinky would not of like that. Then he look in my face.

Why did he leave you? he said.

I look down at the ground. I dunno, I said.

Did he like you? he said.

He like me fine, I said.

Then why did he leave you? he said. People don't leave

people they like, he said. Unless they has a reason. I guess maybe you're mistaken, he said. I guess he didn't really like you.

I look into his face. Tears rolling down mine.

That's not true, I said. He give me a ride, and he bought me them cherries and them grapes. And dinner too, and them clothes. He liked me fine. Just fine. A lot more than Pinky did, I'll bet.

It sure sounds like he liked you a lot, he said. A whole lot. But if he liked you, why did he ran and left you?

I dunno, I said. I guess . . .

You guess what? he said.

Only reason I could think of. I guess 'cause of what he did.

That's what he told you?

I guess.

He took out his book and wrote things down. On and on he asked me questions. And wrote things down.

Simon W. Merton ➤ Sarah is knitting again. Sitting

in the wing chair with the faded flower pattern, beside the drawn curtains. Knitting something dark and indistinguishable, Myrna curled up on the sill beside her. The way she knitted for weeks after Larry was killed at Danang. Three cats ago.

"Time for bed," I say, putting aside the financial page of the *Tribune.*

She rolls her eyes up at me, over her bifocals, without lifting her head from the knitting.

"You go," she says. "I'll be along."

I shrug and climb the stairs, slowly, and get into my pajamas.

When there is no sign of her stirring, I put my dentures in to soak, and ease into bed. I worry for a time, feeling helpless. Thinking of the girl on the lake in 1945. And what has become of her.

"Why don't you go see Dr. Gallenkamp?" I had said earlier in the evening.

"Knitting is no disease," she had replied. "Not of the body, nor of the mind."

And had kept on knitting. The dark thing dropping off her knees already, toward the floor.

I turn over and switch off the lamp beside the bed and go to sleep.

The alarm awakens me.

Sarah's bed is still untouched.

I put on my robe and slippers and go downstairs. She is

asleep in the wing chair, the knitting in her lap. The lamp still on beside her, weak in the morning light.

It has been this way for three nights now.

Belinda Marshall ➤ I drove out the highway with the top down, the wind blowing my hair. I kept to fifty-five, but cars were passing as if I were standing still. That makes me feel like an old lady, at twenty-six. I eased on up, past sixty-five to seventy.

I had scrubbed myself in the shower till I almost bled. Needing to scrub away all traces of him. And took out the diaphragm and stabbed it through with a scissors. Killing all vestige. I'll get a new one. I would never put that one back in.

I dressed still in a rage. Only now, on the highway, with the sun burning my face and the flatland racing by, was it starting to fade.

You're full of shit, Eric. Full of shit.

I tried to remember what I had ever seen in him. I couldn't. It was one of those purely chemical things, I guess, that after it passes leaves no trace.

Like certain poisons.

It began because of Walter, of course. The circumstantial evidence so overwhelming that I wanted character witnesses. To convince the jury that he was not the kind of boy who could do something like that. Perhaps to convince myself as well. I started at the college in Vegas. The basketball coach was helpful. A good kid, he said, no hanky-panky in the locker room. Though he did have to reprimand him on occasion for being late for practice.

The recruiter, Peterson, was of less help. He didn't really know the boy, he said. He couldn't be sure of anything. I crossed him off my list.

Next came his teachers, and Eric was first. We had coffee in the cafeteria. A quiet boy, he said, didn't speak up much in class. He didn't really know him very well. He wished he could be of more help. And how long would I be in Las Vegas—two more days—and would I like to have dinner that night? Why not?

The Strip at night was beyond my wildest imaginings. So super-tacky it was fun. And Eric winning at roulette with reckless abandon, more riverboat gambler than history prof. One thing led to another.

He didn't let on that he was married till the morning.

"I don't let it bother me," he said. "Neither does Estelle."

I made several more trips down there, and he spent some weekends in Salt Lake. Things just sort of developed. Till the trial, when he left her. And switched to the university here, so we could be together.

If only I hadn't taken his advice, the trial might have ended differently.

Just maybe.

I hit the brake with my foot and regained control of the Porsche. Just in time to avoid climbing the back of the Nova ahead.

David Gonzales ➤ If it wasn't me, it would've been somebody else. It's as simple as that.

I was a little early for the ball game, so I stopped at the Red Rock for coffee. A tourist couple with three noisy kids were eating in one of the booths. But the counter was empty. I sipped my coffee and kidded with Marylou. The tourist kids kept glancing at my gun. Marylou kept glancing at the tourist kids. She wanted them out of there so she could start cleaning up. So she could leave at nine o'clock sharp and maybe catch the last half of the game.

The coffee was half gone when a noisy bike roared up outside and a kid came in and sat down at the counter, a few stools away. He ordered a cheeseburger and a Coke. And a side order of fries. A black boy he was, cocoa color and nice-looking, with the natural hair they wear nowadays, only not so big as to be flaunting it. You know what I mean.

No special reason to dwell on what he looked like. It's just that we don't see too many black folks in Grants. A tourist couple once in a while, but that's about it. Even so, he acted so natural, pouring a ton of ketchup all over that burger and fries, that I didn't put it together right away.

Then, taking a sip, I put it together, and nearly spilled the cup.

"Be back in a minute," I said to Marylou, and casually, so's not to alarm him, I sauntered outside. Sure enough, it was a Honda.

I went back in and played with my coffee, letting him finish his food. I was pretty sure it wasn't him. For one main reason. My squad car was parked right outside, big as life. Anyone fleeing the law, he could find a better place to snack than with a police car parked outside.

Of course, like they brought out at the trial, he didn't know he was fleeing the law just yet. Didn't know they were on to him so quick. There was nothing else open, anyway.

When he was finished and paid up and stepping outside, I stepped out after him. I sure as hell was hoping it wasn't him. The ball game would be starting in ten minutes, and Richie would be playing first base. The state regionals, it was.

"Excuse me," I said, real polite. There was no reason not to be. "I'd like to ask you a few questions."

"What about?" he said.

"About where you're headed," I said.

Then I remembered the courts. You got to be careful these days. I told him he could remain silent if he wanted. And that he could get a lawyer, too. He looked all confused right then.

"A lawyer?" he said. "What for? What did I do?"

"Maybe nothing," I said. Pretty sure that was it. "That's what I have to find out. You want to answer my questions?"

"Shoot," he says. A funny choice of words, looking back.

I asked him where he was coming from. Utah, he said. I asked him where he'd spent the night before. A state park, he said. Wasatch Canyon.

Oh, oh, I thought. Us having a nice conversation in the parking lot in front of the Red Rock Diner, with the sun disappearing behind the mesa and a cheer going up at the ball park across town. And this black boy beginning to hang himself.

"Do you have a knife?" I said.

I realized then that I was playing it a bit too cool. Or stupid, to be honest about it. I never even searched him. He could've been packing iron right there.

"A knife?" he said. "Why you want to know that?"

I noticed his accent changing a little then. Getting a little street-tough, the way they show black boys in the movies.

"Just answer the question," I said. Getting a little street-tough myself.

"I bought a knife yesterday," he said. "I lost it in the park last night."

72

Well, that was it. I mean it didn't prove he did anything. But he was the boy they were looking for, all right.

"I'm afraid I got to take you down to the police station," I said. Hearing more cheers from the ball park. Half wishing I had never stopped for coffee.

"What for?" he said.

"I got to make a phone call," I said.

I searched him then, just to make sure. He was clean. I let him ride the bike down the highway, me cruising in the patrol car behind.

The jail was empty that night. I sat him in the office and got his I.D. and checked it out with his wallet. Some college cards, stuff like that. Then I placed the call.

"Briggs," I said. "His name is Walter Briggs."

The lieutenant sounded disappointed when I said that. I didn't know what he expected.

"He was in Wasatch Canyon last night. Says he lost his knife there."

I looked at him, sitting bewildered on the bench.

"It could be the truth," I said. "He seems all right. A college boy. Plays basketball for Nevada-Las Vegas."

"Well, well," the lieutenant says. Just like that. "Well, well." Then he says that's their man. I should hold him for suspicion of murder. They'll be down to get him in the morning.

What could I do? Another state asks you to hold someone, you hold him.

I hung up and booked him. It hurt a bit, too. Either he was innocent or he was the best actor I ever saw. And the cheers coming from down the road.

"You like baseball?" I said.

He said he did.

"If I were to put you in jail right now," I said, "I'd have to sit right here with you. But if you promised not to make trouble, we could go watch a ball game together."

He shrugged his shoulders like I was crazy. We locked his bike in the lobby and went over to the ball park. It wasn't any risk. He had no place to run. If you don't know Grants, New Mexico, it's a spot on the highway, right in the desert.

A couple of people looked at us, but it was a good close game and most folks paid no attention. Richie got two for four, but the Tigers lost, 7–6. It was an unhappy crowd departing.

At the station I put him in the cell. He sat on the bunk with his elbows on his knees and his head between his hands. Looking down at the floor.

"I don't know why I did it," I heard him say.

I was walking away outside the cell, and I stopped dead in my tracks. And nearly fell over.

"What was that?" I said.

He didn't say nothing, but kept looking down. I stood outside the bars. He seemed to have gotten smaller all of a sudden. A trick my eyes played.

"You telling me you killed someone?" I said.

He didn't answer right away. Just kept looking at the floor. He blew out his breath in a long drawn sigh. But when he spoke his voice was clear.

"The knife," he said. "I stole the fucking knife."

I opened the cell and went inside and sat at the end of the bunk. He seemed to be the kind of kid you could talk to.

"Why'd you do that?" I said. Gentle, like a father would be.

He shook his head and dropped his hands from his face. And started in talking, still looking down at the floor.

"I don't know why," he said. "It all happened in a minute. I was in one of those gift shops in Vegas. Looking for a turquoise ring for my mother. A souvenir of the West. The clerk was helping someone else, who was buying a knife. There was two of them out of the glass case. Hunting knives, with turquoise in the handle. I see them out of the corner of my eye, and I think, that would come in handy, camping across country. And then I could give it to my brother as a present. But it must be expensive, I think. And then the two of them move to the back of the store and leave one of the knives right there on the counter. As if made to order. Shit, I thought, I could just lift it and get out of there before they even notice. And I did it, on impulse. Slipped it up my sleeve and left. I guess I was pretty mad at the whole damn town. I thought they owed me."

Him saying all of this still looking at the floor. As if talking made him feel better. In a minute he went on.

"I felt like shit afterward. I never did nothing like that before, except for stealing fruit as a kid. I decided I'd throw it away. But I looked at it up in my room. A real good knife, with turquoise the shape of an eagle in the handle. Leroy would freak out. So I put it in my pack and didn't take it out till after I left town. Till after we crossed the state line. Then I clipped it on my belt, like any camper would."

"And then?"

He looked up at me, for the first time.

"And then nothing," he said. "I lost it in the park."

I nodded. He was through talking, that was for sure. I got up and locked him in the cell. Thinking I shouldn't believe him. But feeling that I did. He didn't seem like no killer to me.

I went and bedded down in the office. In the morning they came for him. One thing I meant to ask them, but I forgot, was what difference his college made. It all came out later on, at the trial.

Virgil LeFontaine ► The balustrade windows are open, sucking in such stray spring breezes as find their way from the river through the twisting streets of the Quarter. The breezes carry the scents of lilacs and whores and the music from Preservation Hall down the block. I step out onto the balcony to listen and to sniff. The wrought-iron railings are filmed with the day's dust. I fetch a clean rag and remove the filth.

Back inside I shed my jacket and bow tie and slip into a dressing gown—the blue brocade. (A gift from Mason.) I fix a Tom Collins with a touch of grenadine, and recline on the chaise longue (picked out by a decorator friend, never mind who. A bit gauche, but I don't want to insult him. You never know). Besides, the cat likes to sleep on it during the day. When she's not out hunting.

The music from the street wraps itself around the wrought iron, mingles with the musk, spills into the room, crawling along the ceiling and the walls, relaxing me as I drink. I went to the place only once. Classic jazzmen stomping and whomping and wailing their Dixieland. An overcute sign on the wall behind them: "Requests, One Dollar. The Saints, Five Dollars." The music enthralls, but the place is so small, the audience packed tightly together on benches, everyone sweating as if in a Turkish bath, ugly beads of sweat rolling down in the lights. Here in the apartment I accept the peace of the horns, the promise of the drums, with none of the drawbacks. Without the salt of contact.

Of life.

Now, now. I mustn't get petulant. And think of Philadelphia. Of little Vinnie Fountain watching the dance of the tenements. Hallway *pas de deux*. Grim fairy tales (a pun, a double pun) of what he will be when he grows up. Smiling through their fat faces.

What do they know of it? What does anyone know of it?

Little Vinnie instead of playing with the others makes puppets from newspaper and paste. And hears things he shouldn't hear. And puts on puppet shows for the younger ones. And just as they are loving and laughing at the puppets most, he smashes them on the stoop. (One day he will play Baltimore, where the stoops are more famous.) The paper heads split open. The little children cry and run away.

(It was only Judy whose mocking head he smashed. Never Punch.)

The puppet shows on Sundays, after church. After Mass, to which Mother dragged me, terrified of the darkness, the candles, the must. Of the dead people on crosses staring down. The air so thick I could hardly breathe. The smell of incense so strong once that I had to run outside, run right down the middle aisle in front of all of them, out into the sunlight, gasping. "No, don't make me go back," I screamed the following week. But she made me go, made me face them. Dragged me by the wrist. The air thicker than ever, eyes on the back of my head, remembering my shame of the week before. (Where was their forgiveness then?) Midway through the service I fainted. And awoke stretched out on a pew in the rear, thinking it was my coffin. With the saints looking down. I never went back again. Except in the trammels of dreams.

The doorbell chimes. It must be Mason. Where is it we're going tonight? The Court of the Three Sisters. Hardly the best food in town, but one of Mason's favorites. I think it's just the name that speaks to him. I will adore it, of course.

He's just a child. But sweet.

Walter Briggs ► Jonesy says it's the funniest thing

he ever heard. But you know Jonesy.

It happened last Sunday afternoon when some new guard I don't know opened the door and let me out and said I had visitors.

"Who?" I said.

"Helping Hands," he said.

"What's that?" I said.

"You'll see," he said.

I followed him down the corridors of empty cells. Me and Jonesy are the only ones just now. The gray paint on the floors of Death Row is less scuffed than in other parts of the prison. Because people here just walk it one time, Jonesy says. Exaggerating. Till we get to the visiting room, which has wooden picnic tables, as if the bars in the windows high up should be trees. The room was empty except for four people sitting together at one of the tables. A man wearing a light blue suit and a white shirt and a blue tie. A woman wearing a green dress. And two children about eight years old, a boy and a girl, all dressed up in their Sunday best. They were white and well-scrubbed and they all sort of looked alike, like a family on the cover of some magazine who just got back from church. I stood there, not knowing what it was about.

"You must be Walter," the woman said.

"Yes, ma'am," I said. Not certain what attitude to adopt.

"Officer, could you wait outside?" the man said.

The guard who I don't know nodded and shrugged and went out to stand in the hall, closing the door behind.

"Have a seat," the man said.

I sat at a picnic table a few feet across from them.

"Well, Walter," the woman said. "Tell us about yourself."

The children sitting with their hands clasped in front of them like they make you do in first grade.

"What for?" I said.

"So we can help you," the man said.

"So we can be friends," the woman said.

I looked from one of their faces to the other. They didn't seem to mean no harm.

"How can you help me?" I said.

The man and the woman looked at each other.

"Perhaps it would be easier if we told you about ourselves first," the woman said. "I'm Clara Maddox, and this is my husband, George. And these are Kenneth and Tracy. I used to teach school. I hope to go back to it someday, when the children are grown. George is an insurance salesman."

"All kinds of insurance," George said, with a big smile. "Burglary, accident, life insurance. I'm not here on business, of course. Though once you're on your feet again, you might think about life insurance. No upstanding citizen should be without it."

They must have escaped from the loony bin. That's all I could think of.

"Would you like to tell us about yourself now?" the woman said. "Or would you rather we sang some songs first and talked afterward?"

"Songs?" I said. They was out of their minds.

"Let's sing, let's sing!" the little girl said.

"Calm down, Tracy," the man said. "We'll get to that. But first I'd like Walter to tell us a little about himself. That's the only way we can be friends when he gets out next month."

Gets out?

"First of all, Walter, what do you think it was about your life that led you to turn to drugs?"

I stood up.

"I think there's some mistake," I said. "I . . ."

Just then the door opened, and another guard walked in with another prisoner, and my own guard behind.

"This is Biggs," the other guard said. "Walter Biggs."

I closed my eyes and smiled.

"But I thought . , ." the woman said.

"I'm afraid there's been a mix-up," the guard who brought me said. "This here is Walter Briggs. Biggs is the one you want."

Biggs was a scrawny-looking guy even younger than me, with red hair and freckles.

"Let's go, Briggs," the guard said to me.

"Well, I don't see . . ." the woman began.

"Now wait a minute," the man said. "We've already started with Walter here. I don't see that it makes a difference that . . ."

"I like the first Walter," the little girl sang out.

With that the Biggs kid exploded. For no reason.

"You dirty . . ." he said, and leaped at me like a cat. The force knocked me over, him grabbing me around the neck, the two of us rolling on the floor. I twisted away from under him and got on top and pinned him, my knees on his arms, and held him there, him struggling, the woman and the kids screaming somewhere above. Till the guards pulled us apart.

"Get him out of here," my guard said to the other. And he pulled the Biggs kid out of the room. I brushed off my pants. Things calmed down a bit.

"Well," the woman said, her face all flushed, "would you like to resume? Or do you think we should let it go until next week?"

I shook my head.

"I don't think you folks can help me," I said.

"Now, Walter," the man said, "selling insurance I get to meet a lot of people. I'm a damn good judge of character. We've worked with prisoners before. There's few men who can't go straight with a little bit of encouragement."

What the hell.

"They're gonna execute me next month," I said.

The man and the woman looked at each other with nervous smiles.

"You shouldn't make jokes like that in front of the children," the woman said.

"Mama, what's execute?" the little girl said.

"That means they're gonna kill him," the boy said.

"Hush up," the woman said. And looked imploringly at the guard. The guard nodded in affirmation.

"Oh, my God," the woman said. "What did he do?"

As if I wasn't there any more.

"He killed a man," the guard said.

The boy's eyes went wide. The girl started to cry and buried her face in her mother's breast. The man stood up.

"Well, I guess there's been a mistake," he said.

"Sorry if it's been any trouble, folks," the guard said. And started moving with me toward the door. At the door I stopped and turned around. I couldn't resist.

"About that life insurance—" I said.

The guard shoved me through the door and closed it behind.

Ha ha ha. Ho ho. Hee hee. Jonesy slapping his knees and banging his head against the bars after I told it to him.

"About that life insurance! Funniest damn thing I ever heard." And laughed and laughed and kept on laughing. "You shoulda bought some for me, too." And he laughed and laughed again. The laughter making an eerie sound in the empty row.

Simon W. Merton ➤ In two days we didn't say more than ten words to each other. You know what that's like with Sarah? That's like ten drops going over Niagara.

She just sat there all evening long, knitting. It wasn't as if she were knitting socks or sweaters or something else useful. Such as a scarf. I'll be needing a new scarf next winter. It wasn't anything like that. It was just knitting. The needles clicking. This long dark thing getting longer and longer, off her lap and halfway across the room. A long dark piece of nothing. An accusation.

Finally I couldn't take it any longer.

"Who the hell do you think you are?" I said. "Madame Defarge?"

She didn't say anything. Didn't even look up from her knitting.

Son of a bitch, I thought. That's exactly who she thinks she is!

Only Sarah's never read Dickens. I know that. Read nothing but religious books in school, and nothing much at all after that. She's a doer, not a reader. Gardening, knitting, crocheting, bargello. Donating them to rummage sales at the church. The money going to charity.

The knitting just that goddamned intuition again. The female intuition for the jugular. Exhibit A being the black widow spider.

Madame Defarge!

Maybe she saw the damn movie on TV.

The note was on the kitchen table when I got home from court the other day:

Dear Simon,

I am moving out of the house for a time. I need to think things through for myself. I am taking an apartment downtown. Please don't try to find me, or there will be no hope for us at all. I will let you know my thinking in about a month, after that boy . . . I will let you know my thinking in about a month.

Don't forget to watch your diet.

Love,
Sarah

Her buff stationery, her ladylike handwriting. At first I was flabbergasted. How could she do this to me? Then I thought: good riddance. I won't have to watch that infernal knitting any more. That hangman's noose, or whatever.

That was three days ago.

I miss her terribly. Much to my surprise.

There's no place I want to go without her. Not just because I'd have to explain her absence. So I sit here alone, not able to concentrate. Feeling as empty as the house. Helpless. Powerless. Staring at the walls.

It's no way for a person to live.

Walter Briggs ➤ Today I had a visitor again. This time it was no mistake. It was Miss Marshall, the lawyer. She wanted to go over everything again.

"Why?" I said.

"Why not?" she said.

So I lived it all again. Going to sleep beside Daralyn, the knife digging into my side. Putting the knife on the seat of the bike while we slept. Rolling the bike away in the early dark, forgetting all about the knife. Till the sun was up and I was half an hour down the highway.

Remembering I don't have the knife. Thinking it must've fallen off in the dark. Thinking I ought to go back.

But if I go back, Daralyn is there. I can't leave her to her face. But I can't take her with me.

The heck with the knife, I decide. And ride on with the sun burning bright.

"Those creakies Daralyn heard," Miss Marshall said.

I always smile when she says that. Sounds like some breakfast cereal. Rice Creakies.

We decided long ago. Those creakies weren't me, like I thought. Those creakies were the killer, stealing the knife. It didn't fall off at all.

Miss Marshall looks like she hasn't slept too good. She sighs and closes her eyes a second and pinches the top of her pretty nose.

"If only you'd gone back," she murmurs. "If only you'd gone back for the knife."

I've thought of that a million times, lying here on the bunk.

If only I'd gone back.
That is the true name of the black man's God. If Only.
Maybe it is the true name of every man's God.

Josephine Briggs ➤ I must've fall asleep after a time, 'cause when the bus man call out Chicago the sun was burning yellow through the windows. One thing I learned early on. No matter what your troubles, the sun comes yellow in the morning. My granddaddy catch his foot in the mowing machine, the sun come up the next day. The barn with all the hay catch fire, the sun come up the next day. Even that summer of the drought, when all the crops was dust and there wasn't no food or work. The dumb sun come up every day. Not knowing it was its own fault.

And later, when Harold left. It keep shining still. Fat lot the sun know about life.

"Chicago," the bus man say.

The fat lady got up.

"Have a good visit with your boy in Utah," she said.

"I certainly will," I said.

I walk down the aisle after her, my suitcase banging on the seats. Maybe I brought too much clothes, but I don't know how long it'll be.

In the terminal I use the ladies' and order a cup of coffee. And wait two hours for the bus to Salt Lake City Utah. The waiting room is long wooden benches, dark brown. Sitting on them some young white boys and girls, college-age type, with suitcase or bright orange backpack things. And the rest a lot of colored folks. About everyone who is not young is colored. I was at Kennedy Airport once, that time I saw Walter off to college. It wasn't like bus terminals. Most folks at the airport was white. The times they are achangin', like the fat lady said. But not as fast as the fat lady thinks.

One time I was supposed to go on a plane myself. When that college was paying to show me the scenery. I was plenty scared. But I took sick with my ankles on a crutch and never got to go. Maybe if Walter gets freed we'll use the money left to fly back home. Together. If.

Like the birds.

Then the new bus is ready. It looks the same as the old. We leave Chicago, which is tall and gray like New York. After Chicago all the buildings stop. The road goes on but on both sides is nothing but flat. It makes you wonder where all the people live. And then the sun is on the other side, and there are wheatfields and cornfields standing green like the cotton-fields in Georgia. We stop in some cities, but they aren't much to speak of. A bus stop and a J. C. Penney and a few buildings three flights high. Without even fire escapes. And a Howard Johnson on the road where we eat.

Dark comes again. The driver says it is the middle of the country, just about half on each side. I think he is mistaken. There are much more people back home. You'd think the whole country would tilt like a seesaw.

I remember how Walter used to play seesaw in the play-ground. One time coming home from work I saw him there, seesawing with some little girl. They both was eight or nine. And a bunch of other little boys sitting on the ground, watch-ing. Every time Walter would touch bottom and the little girl in her pink dress be up, all the other boys would giggle and roll on the ground. I walked over to look. And got all hot in the face. That little girl didn't have her underpants on. Walter tole her to take them off. And every time he was down and she was up, all those boys was lookin' under her dress. And Wal-ter too. I pulled him off that seesaw by his ear and boxed him upside his head real good.

"What kind of game you call that?" I yell at him.

"Seesaw," he says, crying, trying to block my hands from hitting his head again.

"That ain't no way to play seesaw," I say.

"Yes, it is," he say. "You should see what I done saw!"

And laughing through his tears, he dances away, dances all around me, till I have to bite my lip to look stern and keep from laughing myself. He never let you stay mad at him, that boy.

Course, that was ten or eleven years ago. Now you're growed up, people like to stay mad. Even if you didn't do nothin' wrong. Even if it ain't fair. Give people half a chance, they'll get mad at you rather than not. Like my ladies back at home dyin' of dirty house.

I close my eyes with the bus crossing night, and try to get some sleep. Thinking of what to say. And dream bad dreams, as I been having.

Belinda Marshall ➤ I should have joined the Peace Corps. Helped deliver babies in Africa. Something close to the earth. Bodies instead of minds.

Drought. Intestinal parasites. Tsetse flies. A hundred and twenty degrees at night, and one shower a week.

I went to law school instead.

"Attagirl," Dad said.

First in the class at Ogden High.

Summa cum laude at Berkeley.

"Despite the current reaction against reason, in favor of feeling, it is the human mind that distinguishes man from beast. It is the human mind that in the end must save mankind."

From the graduation valedictory speech at Duke Law School by Belinda Marshall.

"Attagirl."

It's all there in the books on the shelves, and these piled here on the desk. The entire history of Anglo-American jurisprudence. And not a paragraph anywhere that will save Walter Briggs.

Do you kill a boy on circumstantial evidence?

That's what it comes down to. To how the Governor feels about that.

Not what he *thinks* about it. How he *feels* about it.

This morning I put my scissors through my diaphragm. The triumph of reason over emotion.

I stand and pace the office. Everyone else is gone. There is a huge forest fire in California. The smoke is drifting in over the Great Salt Lake. My brain is no clearer than the smoke.

Circumstantial evidence. How many times did I review it with Eric before and during the trial?

He stole the knife. The murder weapon. Granted.

"A prior felony," the prosecutor purred. "Evidence of prior criminal tendencies. Evidence of premeditation."

He left the scene in the middle of the night, in a hurry. Granted.

But both could be explained.

The initials. Ah, the famous initials. L period V period. For Las Vegas. His college. The college he was mad at. The college that just took away his scholarship. The college that sent him packing with no money. The college that was ending his dream.

So he carved the college initials in a man's chest?

Bullshit!

"The girl," Eric said. "You're forgetting the girl."

Of course. The girl. A mental retard. Spent half her life in institutions.

"She said he did it."

She did not say he did it! She said he told her he did it. And that was why he was leaving. It's not the same thing.

"To the jury it's the same thing," Eric said.

But why, damn it, why? He had no motive. They haven't said a word about motive! How can they convict? They can see him sitting there. He's obviously not insane.

The prosecutor knew it too. No motive, no case.

The next day he had his motive. Homosexual rage! Jesus H. Christ.

He got the medical examiner to say it.

"Judging by the fact that the victim was unclothed, by the presence of sperm, and by the mutilation of the body, I would say that this was a sex crime, probably committed by a homosexual male."

I objected, of course. Not certain where he was leading. Pure speculation. I asked for a mistrial.

Motion denied.

Then he had Daralyn up there. Telling how she wanted Walter to make love to her, alone in the dark. How she kept touching his pants. How she wanted him to do it, but she couldn't make him stiff.

"I can't," she remembered him saying.

The prosecutor leaped on that.

"Instead, he got up and prowled the park, seeking another outlet. Is that right?"

Objection!

Sustained. The prosecutor will rephrase the question. The jury will disregard the prosecutor's remarks.

Disregard. Ha! I slam down the transcript, furious all over again. The way they kept implying Walter was homosexual, without ever stating it. Knowing they couldn't prove it.

I asked permission to subpoena additional witnesses. Pure bravado. A shot in the dark.

Permission granted.

It was four o'clock Friday. The court adjourned until Monday morning.

Additional witnesses?

A girl friend. I needed to find a girl friend to save his life. Some girl friend!

Leroy Briggs ➤ I sit in the dark room, the rolling TV picture climbing the walls. Waiting till it be time. The phone ring and Angel calls. She wants to come over, she says. She wants to come over with my mama away and have me stick it to her. In your mama's bed, she say. Won't that be fun? We can do it in your mama's bed.

I can't tonight, I say. I got sumpin' else I got to do tonight.

What you got to do, she say. You seein' someone else?

Shit, no, Angel, I doan like no one else but you. It's just this business thing I got to do. I can't say what it is. I doan want you messed up in sumpin' bad.

I messed up bad with you, Leroy Briggs, she say. I want you sweet thing inside me right tonight.

Sheeet!

I want you too, Angel, I swear I do. But this other thing I got to do. Tell you what, I say. Let's us do it right now. Over the phone.

Over the phone? she say. Have you gone crazy, Leroy?

Now listen to me. I'm unzippin' my pants. Wait. I'll put the phone by my pants. There, you hear that. I just unzipped. And now I got it out. It's gettin' big already.

Now you drop those jeans of yours, okay. Go ahead. Just pull 'em off your sweet round ass down to your knees. And your undies too, okay. You do that? Well, okay, she say.

Now you lie down on your bed and stick your finger in. And me on the couch here. Holdin' it with my hand. As if it was your hand. And now we talk to each other. We rub and pull and talk. Tell me about them nipples, standing up stiff now, everything getting all wet.

Oh Leroy Leroy she say into the phone your sweet long thing I want it inside me and stick my finger in your ass in deep way in and out all this little Angel sayin' to me she fifteen years old piece of talkin' on the phone the phone and me talkin' back and oh God Jesus blam . . .

We both breathin' hard, far away.

That okay for you? I say after a time.

That was bad, real bad, she say. You wanna do it again?

I can't, not now, I say. What she think I am? We'll do it again tomorrow.

And hang up the phone, and get a towel from the kitchen to wipe the couch.

I lay back still for a time. Then the news come on the TV, and I know it is time. Time to go.

Down the stairs and into the dark street. Loose and easy. Till I come to the railroad yard where we used to play as kids. Where Walter broke all the windows that time. And climb the fence and walk down the tracks and climb up onto the platform.

No one else is there. No one going no place this late at night. I wait against the back in the shadows. Then up the track the light is coming, far away. It doan seem to be moving. But little by little it gets closer. Then faster and faster. Then the train is rushing into the station.

I stay behind a pole and wait. The train slows, it stops. Dim yellow bulbs inside. Maybe two, three people in each car.

The doors pull back with a whoosh. A man getting out the far end. A lady getting out this end. I look up and down. No one else.

The man is gone now up the other steps. The woman coming this way. A black lady. Damn.

I got no choice.

She walks by. I step out behind the pole and grab her bag. Wha!

I jump off the platform where the train just been, and run along the tracks, the train lights running faster up ahead. I hear her yelling, but there ain't no one to hear her nohow. I cross the yard and up the gravel slope and climb that chain-linked fence. And shove her bag inside my jacket and cross

93

the street. And walk two blocks home real slow. Slow and easy.

Up the stairs I go, into the apartment. And go into the bathroom and turn on the light. A cockroach run away.

I open that brown bag of hers. Lipstick, comb, tissues, all kinds of junk. No wallet anywhere.

Then I find a small black purse. Inside a small roll of bills. My fingers shake as I unroll the roll to count.

Seven dollars. All ones.

And forty-nine cents in change.

And two subway tokens.

Sheeet!

That ain't enough for nothin'.

I put the money in my pocket. I take her bag and go inside and shove it under the bed. Way back against the wall among the dust.

Ain't no other way. Tomorrow I got to take a knife.

Belinda Marshall ➤ Darkness has fallen like lead over the city, speeded by the smoke from California. The street lights from the window fade to a yellow haze in a matter of blocks. I stuff the transcript into my bulging briefcase and zip it up. Sven, the elevator man, is polite as always.

"Working late again, Miss Marshall?"

Translation: Still trying to save that nigger-boy?

I toss the briefcase onto the seat, and drive. Past the Tabernacle, past the Convention Center. Downtown is deserted at night, as always. More like a small town than a major city.

Driving tickles some thought in my brain. Some thought I had in the morning, driving away from Eric, driving out to the prison to see Walter. Some thought that remains beyond reach. That I know I don't want to reach.

I rerun a conversation in the jail two years ago. The day after the homosexual stuff. Walter sitting at the picnic table with his head down, looking for the first time utterly beaten.

"How you doing?" I said.

He didn't answer. His head hanging.

"Come on, Walter," I said, putting my notes on the table. "You can't give up now."

At first he didn't respond. Then he looked up at me, his eyes bigger and more soulful than ever. When he spoke his voice was anger with all the tension melted out. A broken spirit.

"Why'd he say those things about me?"

I sat across from him. Summoning my bravest front. Not-so-brave Belinda, out of her league.

"Is that what you're worried about? Walter, I'm surprised at you. Courtroom games, that's all that was. We'll knock it down to nothing."

"Oh, yeah? So why did you object? I'll bet it's in all the papers."

"Listen to me. Look at me. That's better. I objected because he was playing dirty. That's not allowed. Also to have grounds for appeal, in case we lose. And he just gave us a whopper. Only we aren't gonna lose. We're gonna knock him flat next week. As for the papers, we're not trying the case in the papers. The jury is all that counts."

Attagirl, Belinda. I could see a bit of his hope coming back. Tentative.

"How we gonna knock 'em flat?"

"Okay," I said. "He implied you're homosexual. That's nonsense, right."

Walter smiled. If I could read what he was thinking, he would have liked to show me, not tell me. It hung in the prison air for just a jot. We both let it pass.

I took out my pen and a pad.

"All I need," I said, "is the names of some of your girl friends. Names and addresses. Girls you've dated at school." I hesitated, then continued. "Girls you've slept with, preferably. We'll put them on the stand. Poof. No more motive. No conviction."

Walter looked at me, a puzzled squint in his eyes. Something warned me of trouble on the way.

"Girls?" he said.

"Yes, girls. What else?"

He looked down again, saying nothing.

"Walter, I know you don't like to kiss and tell. But this isn't frivolous. It's a court of law. Someone was murdered, and as long as they think it's you, they won't look for anyone else. And the real killer could kill again. Surely the girls would understand that. People's lives are at stake."

Without mentioning his own. Neat, Belinda, if I say so myself.

Still he said nothing.

"Well?"

Still looking down. Mumbling now more than speaking.

"I was busy studying. And with basketball practice."

Oh oh.

"I was just a freshman. Most of the girls at school was older than me."

The room began to spin for just a second. I clung tight to the table.

"You mean you didn't go out with girls? You didn't go out on dates?" The floor dropping away below me. Keep plugging, Belly. "Not that that's a crime. Lots of boys . . . young men . . . are late developers, as they say. Lots of perfectly normal boys don't start dating till they're seniors. Or later."

Walter looking down. Saying nothing.

"But you have to tell me the truth. One way or the other. You've never slept with a woman? Yet?"

His eyes came up at last. His voice soft.

"I didn't say that."

The room settled. My breasts were heaving under my blouse. I realized that between sentences I had been holding my breath.

"What, then? You've got to tell me the truth, Walter. It's the only way I can defend you."

He looked at me at last, his face twisted in an agony that I couldn't fathom. Then suddenly relaxing as he made his decision to tell me.

"She's married," he said.

"Oh." My own voice small now. A mixture of relief and consternation.

"And she's white."

I shook my head and smiled. My nervous smile. I was defending a comedian. Only he was dead serious.

I closed my eyes and took a deep breath. And opened them and smoothed my skirt.

"Two complications we really didn't need," I said. "But we can live with them."

"There's something else," he said. He was looking at the table again.

I thought it was time for a joke. Lighten the atmosphere.

"I know," I said. "You were sleeping with the dean's wife."

Walter didn't laugh. Instead he shook his head.

"It wasn't the dean," he said. "Just a professor."

Just a professor! The boy was positively amazing.

"Okay," I said. "Before the plot thickens any more, give me her name. Remember, it's life or dea . . ."

"Estelle," he said. "Est . . ."

"Est . . ."

I started to repeat the name. My mouth dropped open.

"Estelle Hawthorne," he said.

I looked into his face. The pen slipped from my hand. I started to speak, but I couldn't. I started to laugh, but I couldn't. I started to cry, but I couldn't. Then all of a sudden I was laughing and crying at the same time, my head buried in my hands on the table. I don't know how long it was. Till Walter, shaken, came around and put his hands on my shoulders.

Him comforting me!

It brought me out of it, like a slap in the face.

"What is it?" he said. "You know her?"

I found a tissue in my bag and wiped away the tears. Tears of joy—and horror. We had ourselves a witness.

Or did we?

"I know her husband," I said.

Eric. Sweet Jesus. I was having dinner with Eric that night.

Daralyn Kirk ➤ The grass is green and the buildings is white and the water when they take us swimming on the beach is gray. Not blue like they used to tell us then in school but gray and salty in your mouth when it slaps your face. Only now it is raining so they won't take us down to the beach. I look out the window and the sky is gray like the sea far away by the beach. And the window cryin' with the rain. And the white light comes and tries to grab me through, and the thunder after like the roof is falling down. And I run away from the window before it can. If you stand too close to windows it pulls you through. And you can't never come back again. Like them.

I sit on the bed and pull out my coloring book. I make the grass green and the big house white and the water by the sailboat blue, like it ought to be. And the boy on the bike I make brown. Like him.

He is far away looking through right now at the other side of the rain. Through windows with bars on them so it can't pull through. Because of what I said. That's what my friend Michael Maller say. They lock him up in jail 'cause of what I said.

I wish I could go to the other side of the rain and get him free. Just go and give him a gun and get him out. And ride with him on his bike like a shiny black horse. Like we did before. Just ride and ride till we come to a beach where the water is green as grass. And clean and never salty on your face. And lie with him together me and him. In the naked sun all yellow and warm all over. Beyond the reach of nurses and them and it.

They said if I said it right wouldn't be no nurses. If I said it right I could go wherever I please. So I said it right and then they locked him up. And put me with the nurses though they said.

I think I will write a letter. Tell him I am sorry and will come with a gun one day to get him out. And will ride off together on his bike where the water's green, and both be happy together me and him. I take my book all black and white on the cover like the books we wrote in in school away back then. And write my letter on a page and pull it out. And another page comes out too, at the back. And finish my letter on the second page and pull it out. Another page falls out way at the back. I fold the pages and lick the envelope, and give it to the pretty nurse to mail. How quick will he get it, I say. In three or four days, she say. And then it is time to eat and we go to the long benches and there is bread with jam and peas and beans and a carton of milk and fruit in a plastic dish. And when I get back to my room them pages that fell out have blowed down onto the floor. I don't know why it should be when you pull out a page in the front another page comes out in the back, where you can't even see. I don't know why it be but it always is.

Belinda Marshall ➤ When I get home the coffee cup is still on the table from the morning. And the broken toothbrush. And the magazine on the floor. The bed unmade, the blankets twisted as if by a torturer.

Screw it. I never claimed to be a homemaker.

Luckily there is leftover casserole in the fridge. I put it in the oven to warm, and straighten up a bit. The broken toothbrush I begin to throw in the garbage, then stop. It will sit there for two days. Some ceremony seems appropriate. Like a burning.

But the stench would be awful.

I flush it down the toilet instead.

Love is . . .

I put my pad on the table, to make notes for the last appeal. Mercy. Doubts and mercy.

I cross out mercy. Mercy implies guilt.

Doubts. Doubts and circumstances and Daralyn and the possibility of error. Error that the state in all its majesty would not be able to correct. Error that would stain the flag of Utah with innocent blood for all time to come.

Go to it, kid.

I remove the casserole with potholder gloves. Eggplant casserole, with cheese and walnuts. A touch of Proust. Eggplant and memories. It's the same casserole I served Eric that night two years ago. The night Walter dropped his bombshell about Estelle.

We had finished eating. Were sitting in the living room, on the sofa. Sipping cognac. My brain a whirling washing ma-

101

chine of dirty underwear. The most difficult moment of my life.

"You're joking," he said.

His face ashen white beneath the beard. Knowing I wouldn't joke about something like that.

He stood and paced the room. He finished the cognac and splashed more into his glass, spilling some. The spot still there today on the rug.

"The cunt!"

I didn't know what to say. This kind of thing wasn't covered in Moot Court.

"Black bastard cock!"

Sweet Belinda. Over her head again. I should have majored in home ec.

"It's not as if she's alone," I said. "There's us."

His eyes blazing at me.

"That's different!"

"Why is it different? Because she's a woman?"

Go ahead, say it, Eric. The one thing that could possibly make it different. "Because I love you." Say it. I dare you.

"It's just different, that's all."

Tilt!

For half an hour he must have paced the room while we talked. His professor's brain boiling with rage and possibility. Hearing me out, interrupting, hearing me out again.

"If I put her on the stand it will be awful for you. I could just refer to it in summation. No names. Tell of this woman he is protecting. Maybe get sympathy for him that way. And leave Estelle out of it."

"They'll eat you alive," Eric said. "This phantom lady. This phantom lover. Where is she, who won't even come forward to save her lover's life? Or does she exist at all, outside the fantasy of the worthy defense counsel, desperate for an argument? Can't you just hear it?"

He was right.

"Oh, Eric, it's so awful. How you'll suffer if I call her! One of your own students."

He stopped pacing and went to his jacket in the closet. He

got a cigar and lit it. His demeanor had changed suddenly. He had grown calmer. A sort of crazed calm, I remember thinking, but that was an exaggeration.

"You've got to put her on the stand. It's the only way to save your client."

It was what I wanted to hear. But I still wasn't certain myself. I didn't want to put Eric through that. I told him so again. He sat beside me on the sofa, puffing the cigar, drinking more cognac.

"Shit, Belinda, why kid ourselves? He's not the first one. I know it, she knows it, the whole school knows it. The jock-of-the-year club. Estelle Hawthorne's Most Valuable Layer. Might as well make it official. I'll leave her, that's all. The outraged husband. Then we'll be able to see more of each other."

He stood and paced again, the cognac splashing.

"I should have done it a long time ago. Left her or kicked her out. I'll tell her tomorrow. Then you get a subpoena."

"I don't know," I said.

He sat beside me and put the glass down, and the cigar, and put his hands on my shoulders. And looked into my eyes.

"Belly, you took an oath. That boy's life is at stake. I'm surprised you have any doubts at all."

Warmth flooded through me. I hugged him. I covered his face with kisses. His nose, his ears, his beard. He reeked of cigars and drink. I kissed him anyway. I bubbled over.

"And maybe you could transfer to the university here next year. And we could be together all the time."

"That might be possible," he said. "Leave that whole stinking campus behind."

And held me tight.

My man.

My sweet, strong, generous man.

I finish the casserole and put it in the sink. I put up a pot of coffee. My sweet, strong, generous man. Two years it took me to flush his toothbrush down the toilet. Two goddamn years!

I put her on the stand, all right. Like a magician producing a rabbit. Walter's lover. His savior. Shooting down the homosexual claptrap in ten minutes. Going easy on the details. Just the basic facts. Just enough to make the point. They had slept together for three months.

The jury rapt, astonished.

Some homosexual!

Attagirl, Belly.

The cross was more sordid, of course. They made sure to bring out every messy detail. And harped on the fact that Estelle was always the aggressor. That Walter always seemed a little scared.

As if that made him homosexual!

They haven't got a motive left, I thought. Put the champagne on ice.

Instead they put Walter on ice.

Guilty!

How could that be, with no motive?

And then the awful realization, looking at the pinched faces of the jurors as they stared at him. As if he were lower than a worm. Those bland nice lily-white Mormon faces. Motive? They didn't need a motive. This black boy from the East had been sleeping with a white woman! With a married woman! With one of his own professors' wives! The horror. The outrage. Why, anyone who could do that . . . anyone who could stoop so low . . . any black boy who could violate God's law like that . . . why, he could be guilty of anything. He admitted he stole the knife. What for, if not to use it? Who says he couldn't cut up that man in the park? He probably did it with pleasure. He was there, it was his knife, he ran . . .

Guilty as charged.

I still tremble at the memory.

It was I who was the guilty one. Guilty for putting her on the stand. There must have been some other way. Eric couldn't know. Eric isn't a lawyer. But I am. I should have known the jury would be horrified, would react like that. I didn't think. Facts, that's all I thought about. That's all they tell you about in law school.

Everyone knows cases aren't decided on facts!

My whole body is sweating, thinking of it. Reliving it. And

now I am reduced to this. To writing a last-minute appeal.

I leave the table and go to the bathroom and wash my face. The underarms of my dress are soaked. I take it off and pull on jeans and an undershirt. One of those little-girl undershirts I buy at Penney's for a dollar, and dye yellow or green or purple. The coolest thing around the apartment in the late June heat.

I take my pad and curl up on the sofa, barefoot, to make notes for the appeal. I try to write. But I can't concentrate. A tickle is needling my brain. Growing to an irritation. Then to an inflammation. Some evil thought I have been repressing. Trying to break through now.

A devil's egg. Hatching.

Josephine Briggs ➤ My backside was sore when the bus come into Salt Lake City Utah the second night. Purple mountains loom on two sides, with gray buildings standing down in the center. The mountains like pictures in books from far away. I guess I have come far away, but by bus it doesn't seem real. My thoughts are still the same as in the Bronx.

I bump the suitcase off the bus and out into the street. The air is warm and dry, like bread baking in the oven. Somewhere nearby is my Walter, I can feel it thumping in my chest, but I don't know which direction. And up the street a hotel marked "Transients." Hotels near bus stations always are the cheapest. All colored folks know that. Especially hotels marked "Transients."

The room is twelve dollars cash, which seems a lot for cheap. I pay from my purse and bump the suitcase up. The carpet on the stairs is dirty and torn, and the rug in the room also. There is a window I open for air, but only a gray brick wall across the way. "Transients" means they got gray brick walls across the way.

I open my suitcase which is starting to tear on the end and take out my black dress and hang it in the closet on a hanger that is attached. I kick off my shoes and stretch out on top of the bed. A narrow bed with a shelf above your head, on the shelf a black Bible, for later. The bed is soft and sags down in the middle. After two days on that bus it feels real good. In the middle of the room the light bulb on a string burns white. My eyes close hot on the bulb, thinking of different hotels, in fancy parts of town, all painted white with pillars outside, with midgets in red coats and gold buttons to carry your bags. Yes, ma'am, and no, ma'am. Looking like Johnny Philip Morris, in the bypast days with Harold, long ago. Doormen in uniform opening the doors and waiters in black tux and tie and fancy ladies in ball gowns and fancy gentlemen in white suits and gold-handle walking sticks. White wood hotels with ivy on the walls and gardens leading up and back rooms for poker and cigars. In each town across the South the fanciest hotel in town. That's where Harold and his group would play them days. Nothing but the fanciest hotel in town. Then when he was finish late at night we would get in the band bus and drive back across the railroad tracks to niggertown near the station. And peeling paint hotels marked "Transients."

What was it Walter call him? "The King of the Horns."

Harold tole Walter all about them fancy dan hotels. 'Cept the part about going crosstown at night. I think now maybe he should've tole him.

That bulb burning through to my eyes. I get up and pull the string and turn on a lamp near the bed. And go to pull the shade down on the window, but the shade's rolled all at the top and won't come down. I look outside but there's no one there can see. Only the gray brick wall peeking back, flashing red, on and off, from some sign somewheres out front. I go in the bathroom and wash off the two days of bus and put my pink nightgown on. I am hungry but too tired to go eat. I take that Bible down from the shelf and read:

The Lord is my shepherd; I shall not want.

In the morning I will ask where that prison is where they is keeping Walter. And go see him. And then go see the Governor and tell him Walter is a good boy who ain't never been in trouble and couldn't do nothing like that. And they should let him go. No use thinking now 'bout what I will say. A time like that a mother's words come.

Yea, though I walk through the valley of the shadow of death, I will fear no evil.

I put the Good Book away after a time and pull back the covers of the bed. Ain't no bugs to see, thank the Lord. "Transients" is Spanish for bugs. I climb in and put off the light. The room is black except for the red fire blinking from the sign in front.

I lie still in the bed, my bones feeling shriveled, and hear the mountains looming up outside. I say to myself, Josephine Larner Briggs, I guess you have come a long way after all.

But it don't really feel like me inside of me.

I think again of Walter as a chile. One time while I was peeling onions for a stew he make up another one of those 'landish stories of his. There is a place, he say, where everybody cries all the time. Day after day, week after week, nobody can stop their crying. Men and women and even the little children and the babies in their cribs. Everybody cries. Sometimes they feel real bad. Sometimes not so bad. It don't matter. Everybody cries. Sometimes the sun is shining, sometimes it rains all day. But it don't matter which. Everybody cries all the time. Just 'cause that's the way it is.

"Shoot," Leroy say. "I ain't never heard of that. What's the name of that place?"

"Onion City," Walter say.

And smiled all proud of himself.

I shake my head from side to side on the pillow in the dark. Remembering how I smiled along, back then.

Belinda Marshall ➤ He knew! This newborn thing. Ripping at the bowels of dead love like a hyena.

He knew how the jury would react!

The pad has slipped to the floor, the pencil lost somewhere among the cushions of the couch, lost the way household items get lost around the house, impossibly and yet irrevocably; the way love once fled is fled impossibly but forever.

"You've got to put her on the stand. It's the only way to save your client."

Bullshit. It was all bullshit. Double revenge, he was getting. Revenge on both of them. By making her confess to her sins in public. By sending him to his death!

Eric Hawthorne, prelate of history. Lord High Executioner. Judge and jury both, here in my living room.

For the wrong fucking crime!

Unable to sit still, the blood like red ants under my skin, I pace the rug where he paced then. How sadistically he paced! As filled with evil as the killer stalking with Walter's knife toward his victim. And me not noticing. Blinded by the blossoms of love. Becoming his ignorant accomplice.

I go to the cabinet, try to pour a Scotch. I can't. My hands are shaking. The bottle clinking against the glass, and nothing coming out.

Frustrated, I set the bottle down, too close to the edge. I turn, and it thumps to the rug, spurting a malicious spreading stain.

I hurl myself onto the sofa, as if it were a pool in which I could drown. And lie facedown, tears streaming down my cheeks, filling my nose, my mouth. Unable to stop myself, I pound the rug beside the sofa until my fist is raw. Imagining his face beneath me. Until the boiling energy is cooled.

Still I can't relax. I get up and scurry about, looking for a tissue, to blow my nose, to wipe my eyes.

Calm down, I tell myself. Maybe I'm wrong. Maybe the strain of this last appeal is too great. Maybe I'm hysterical.

But a bare skull grins at me. It grins from the ceiling, from the cabinet, from the stain on the rug. I close my eyes and still I see it grin. It grins from the casserole in the sink. From the robe in my closet. From the bracelet in my drawer.

He knew.

And carried that knowledge within him all this time. In his heart. In his brain. In every part of him.

The bare skull grins from the bed.

Oh, God . . .

Leroy Briggs ➤

The phone ring. I doan answer. It might be Angel. I ain't in the mood. No way.

I go to the kitchen and open the drawer and take a knife. The kind we use for steak once a month.

This night I need a man. Maybe two.

I lie on the couch in the living room with the TV flickering in the dark. The black bar cutting off heads.

Like they used to do to kings.

Le Roi.

Walter was good in school. Not me. How they expec' you to read all that stuff? What good is reading books do anyhow? Doan get you money and it doan get you laid. Nohow.

Look where them books got Walter.

On the tube a police car is chasing another car, on a curvy mountain road. Zoom and zoom they go. The TV flickering. And the first car can't turn quick enough, and go sailing off the cliff. The police car stop just in time, hanging near the cliff. The policeman watch the other car crash down below and explode in flames. The policeman shaking his head like he is sorry.

Sheeet!

Then the news come on. I know it is time. I get up and slip it in my pocket. Careful I don't get cut.

Quiet down the stairs and through the streets. Till I climb the fence and down on the platform as before. Waiting in the shadows. Till the train eye come down the tracks.

Rubber doors open. A man get out alone.

Hot dog!

I wait till the train doors close. Till the train starts moving.

111

Then I hurry up behind and grab his arm.

"Gimme your wallet," I say.

"Hey, what is this?" he say, twisting around.

He is not too big. I could take him good.

"Listen, fella," he say, holding some brown 'taché case.

I reach in my pocket and pull it out. Smooth and easy.

"Gimme your wallet," I say, "you doan wanna get cut."

He see the blade low near his belly.

"Take it easy," he say. "Just take it. Take anything you want."

He hand me the 'taché case. I slap it down. He reach behind.

"Slow," I say.

He pull it out slow and give it to me.

"Now turn and start walking," I say.

He turn and start walking.

I pull the money out. And toss the wallet after.

"Here's your wallet," I say.

No harm in being nice.

And think, my brother Walter thanks you. But doan say it. I leap into the tracks and run down. Till I'm out of sight behind the yard, and climb back over and walk home.

In the bathroom two cockroaches run. I count the money in my pocket. Fifty-three dollars cash.

And say it out loud.

"My brother Walter thanks you."

I see my face in the mirror.

Tomorrow I call Cheater Charlie.

Simon W. Merton ➤ I sit in the wing chair, the newspaper unread in my lap. The cat has run away. I don't much care.

If there is one thing I have learned in my sixty-two years, in my twenty-three years on the bench, it is that most people find it difficult to cope with living. The tide of events sweeps over them in the sea of daily life. They wind up floundering and thrashing about.

That is why we have rules, laws. To provide a structure, a framework, in which people can live. To provide guardrails, so to speak. To keep them from drowning.

The system is not perfect, of course. Many people soon wind up over their heads. The rich ones go to psychiatrists. The poor ones go to prison.

I did not make the rules. They are the collective wisdom of mankind, handed down through the centuries. But those of us in each generation who are most able to cope are chosen to enforce the rules. We become the policemen, the lawyers, the district attorneys.

And the wisest among us become the judges.

That is not to say, however, that we have a great deal of discretion. The rules are the rules. We are just the interpreters. The commentators and annotators of the Bible, so to speak. But not its authors.

That is what people too often fail to understand.

Even Sarah, after all these years.

Take that boy, for instance. The rules say that if you are guilty of hacking a man to death with a hunting knife, and if the jury does not recommend mercy, then you must be sentenced to die. There are no ifs, ands, or buts. No discretion.

For a time, of course, we did not have the death penalty in Utah. In those days the boy would have been sentenced to life in prison. Those were the rules.

Now the rules have been changed, by the collective wisdom of the people, speaking through their legislators, and through the Supreme Court of this country. And the rules must be enforced, or we will all drown together.

But what about that girl, people have asked me. What about the time last year when she changed her testimony?

What about it? You see, she did not change her *testimony*. That is sloppy use of the language. Whereas civilization rests on precise use of the language.

What happened is that a newspaperman—Michael Maller, I think his name was—from the Miami *Herald*, befriended the girl in that home for the retarded. He began to visit her each week. And soon he got the story he was after. (He was, of course, using her.) She told him that she had said false things at the trial. She told him Walter Briggs never told her he had killed that man. At the trial, of course, she had remembered him telling her that. That was why he had run away and left her alone in the park. Now, a year later, she was recanting. The newsman printed the story, and it was carried on the national wires. And the lawyer, Marshall, asked for a new trial, on the grounds that a key witness had changed her story.

People seemed to expect that I would grant a new trial, just like that. But they didn't think it through. And they didn't understand the rules.

In the first place, the girl testified under oath. Now, when she was changing her story, she was not under oath. She could say anything, with no consequences. That was not new evidence. For a new trial, you need new evidence, not a change in memory.

But suppose I had ordered a new trial. And suppose, under oath, she then said the boy was innocent. What would that prove? The score would be one for each side. What would we do then? Have a third trial? Best two out of three?

You see what I'm driving at? You can't run a system of

justice haphazardly. Evidence, that's what's important. We can't order new trials every time a witness has pangs of remorse. The rules don't permit it. If they did, there wouldn't be any rules.

You'd think a woman as smart as Sarah would understand that.

I get up and go into the kitchen and make a cup of tea.

What I miss most is not her voice or her smell, but some elusive proof. I feel like a man standing in bright sunlight (the sunlight of my career, if you will) and looking all around and not seeing his shadow. And thus in an unsettling way doubting his own existence.

It's foolishness, of course.

I go to the refrigerator. We seem to be out of lemon.

Walter Briggs ➤ The guard lets me out in the yard

to exercise. Not that nasty Jackson, but the new one. The nice one. Shooting baskets for an hour with cat's eyes looking down from the wall.

The crowd is screaming their heads off. We're down by a point with four seconds left to go. I steal the ball with my lightning-quick hands and I break upcourt. The clock is running and I can't make it in for the lay-up. I stop outside the key and as if in slow motion I bend my knees and go on up for the jumper. The knees bent, the back arching, the right hand pulling back, the left hand steadying the ball. The way I've done a thousand times since I was nine. A million times. The left hand comes under the ball, the right hand starts forward. The crowd a tunnel of roar. And in my head this crazy thought leaps. That if I make this shot my daddy gonna come home.

The arm finishing forward, the wrist snapping, the ball rolling off my fingertips. Rolling off straight and true so that I know as soon as it leaves my hands it's gonna swish. Not even touch the rim but swish clean through. I know it and the ball arcing like a full moon rising and hanging in the roar of the crowd and the buzzer goes as I touch the floor and the ball coming down again, clean and true, swish, and the cords jumping and me jumping and everybody banging my head and the crowd gone wild. We win the city champs, and my daddy's coming home!

And then that referee waving his hands across the floor. What is he waving? I don't believe it! Waving it doesn't count, that I shot after the buzzer. But that is wrong, I know it, I swear it, I heard the buzzer clear with the ball in the air like a full moon rising. And him yelling no and me shouting in his face and others too and hands pulling me away and the crowd a different roar now. And then me in the locker room kicking things down. Busting up my knee.

It still hurts sometimes, out in the yard.

Daddy never come home.

That's pretty dumb, Walter, pretty dumb.

As if he would.

Then the hour is up, and I go on back inside.

"How'd it go, champ?" Jonesy says.

Jonesy's taken to calling me champ since they let him watch me play once.

"Pretty good," I say. "Ain't hard to win when there's nobody playin' against you."

"For some people that ain't true," Jonesy says.

I think about that for a while. Sometimes I can't tell whether Jonesy's making a joke or making you think.

"You goin' out to play?" I say.

"Not me," he says. "The game's all over, sports fans."

Three days. Jonesy gets it Monday.

"I've worked up my last sweat," he says. "Be plenty of time to sweat where I'm goin'. Now if they had a swimming pool, champ, that would be different. A swimming pool to cool off in."

I don't say nothing. What can you say to something like that?

Monday.

I can't stand to think of it.

I think of a black stain spreading on his ceiling too. He never mentioned it.

I never mentioned mine.

He told me once about growing up on a ranch in Montana. Helping his father with the cattle, and his mother dying. Jonesy bringing a girl friend back from the town one day, to live with. And coming back with the cattle one day and hearing screaming coming from the barn, and rushing in and there is his father in the hay on top of his girl. Her screaming to break free. And him grabbing a rifle from the pickup truck and running in and sticking the rifle in his father's ear. The barrel right in his ear, and telling his father to get off, real slow. Which he did, the gun still in his ear, and the girl running off to the house, her clothes all torn. Him sweating but real cool, his father's pants down around his ankles, and Jonesy knowing it would be real easy to squeeze that trigger and blow his father's head. Real easy, he said. He just held it there for a time, his father's naked knees starting to knock. Then he takes the rifle down and goes outside, and throws it into this big old pond they got. And he goes in and throws his clothes in a duffel, and drops the girl back in town and drives off down the highway to never come back. To make his fortune in the cities of the East.

That's what he says, anyway.

Monday.

He killed three people.

He's a real good friend.

Josephine Briggs ➤ In the morning I put on my black dress and have coffee in the bus station down the block. The last time I wore it was to Cora's Mitchell's funeral. Bus drivers having coffee and people with suitcases going every which way. My money in my purse and my shoe. Only fools leave money in "Transients."

I ask the information lady what bus to take to the prison. She has blond hair and a nice blue cap. The prison is not in Salt Lake City, she tell me, but twenty miles out of town. After all that. How they expect folks to visit folks they put prisons way out of town? There ain't no bus that goes.

I go to a telephone booth and call up to make sure. The prison is twenty miles from town, all right. How's a body to get there, I ask the man. Automobile is the only way, he say. How's a body to get an automobile, I say. Can't help you there, he says.

What hours is visiting, I say. Sunday afternoon, he say. Two to six Sunday afternoon. That's the only time, I say. That's the only.

Two to six on Sunday I can see my son.

And no automobiles.

And this be Friday.

I go back to the blond cap lady. Which bus to the Governor's house, I say. The Governor's house? she say. Where the Governor works, I say. Oh, you mean the state capitol, she say. If that's where he works then that's where I mean, I say. Walk down two blocks, she say, and take the whichnumber bus. You'll see it on the top of the hill.

Which I do. The purple mountains pretty in the daytime

119

light. Things that scare you in the night is always less scary in the day. Except some things. The land on the other side stretching like an ocean far and flat as the bus goes up the hill.

"State capitol," the driver call out.

I get off the bus and walk along the walks. Flowers is planted everywhere along the way. Red and yellow and orange and every color. Like at the place across from the zoo I went to with the boys once by mistake. Them wanting to see lions and elephants. Us seeing roses and little begonias by mistake. Walter all upset. Him wanting to see tigers and monkeys and things. And little Leroy whining and crying to wake the dead. This ain't the zoo, him saying. You promised. Till Walter can't stand his crying no more than me. There's the elephants, he say, showing him marigolds. And look at the big giraffes, he say, pointing to some trees. Leroy stop crying and look with big wide eyes. Walter can't keep himself from laughing. Leroy start crying again. Till we get out of there and take a taxi to the zoo. A taxi, for land sakes!

Ahead is the capitol house, all white with columns like the fancy hotels in the South. Only stone, not wood. I go up the steps and into a big wide lobby. A guard with a gun is sitting at a desk. I ask where the Governor's office be. He point me the way, down the lobby and turn.

In the office is a lady at a desk. She ask me what I want. I want to see the Governor, I say. Do I have an appointment, she say. I don't, I say. But I need to see him anyway. Well, I don't know, she say. Can you tell me what it's about? It's about the Governor's gonna kill my son, I say.

She look up at me then sort of nervous. And slide back from her desk half slow. Like she's afraid to make a move. Please wait here just one moment, she say. Extra sweet. Molasses on her tongue.

She go in a back room. I look at pictures on the walls. Different men under glass in wood frames. Then a man come out in a tall gray suit, with the lady behind and goes back to her desk.

"I'm John McPhee, the Governor's press secretary," the man say. "Can I help you?"

"I need to see the Governor," I say.

"What's this about the Governor killing your son?" he say.

"It's true," I say.

"I don't really think . . ." he say.

"My boy in the state prison," I say. "They gonna kill him two weeks from Monday. Unless the Governor say no."

"I see," he say. "And your name is?"

"Briggs. Mrs. Josephine Briggs."

"Oh, yes, of course," he say. "Michael Briggs's mother."

"Walter," I say.

"What?"

"Walter Briggs. Not Michael."

"Yes, of course," he say. "But the judge and the jury have spoken in the case. It's not really the Governor's place to . . ."

"The Governor can stop it if he wants," I say.

"Well, technically that's true," he say. "But only . . ."

"Technically they is gonna kill my boy," I say.

The man look around. The secretary lady is looking up, listening.

"Let's go into my office," the man say. And lead me to a back room. He gives me a chair and sit behind a desk. On the wall in back of him a big oil picture looking down.

"Is that the Governor?" I say.

"Yes, it is," he say.

I look up at the picture. The face round and sort of pink. The hair thin. The eyes with glasses on. A blue suit and a blue tie and a white shirt and an American flag behind him. The eyes telling nothing, neither good or bad. Not from the picture, anyway.

"Now, Mrs. Briggs," the man say. "Your son has a lawyer, doesn't he?"

"Yes," I say.

"Well, I'm sure his lawyer will file a final appeal asking for clemency. The appeal will contain all the pertinent facts and arguments. And the Governor will be able to make a just decision."

I look down at my purse and then at him.

"A lawyer ain't a mother," I say.

Then it his turn to be squirmy.

121

"No, that's true," he say. "But . . ."

"I want to see the Governor myself," I say.

The man stand up.

"I'm afraid that's impossible," he say. "The Governor is very busy today. He has a full schedule."

"Tomorrow, then."

"I'm afraid he's booked up tomorrow, too."

"I come all the way from New York," I say. "On a bus."

"I understand that, Mrs. Briggs," he say. "But I'm afraid I can't help you."

I stand up now, getting angry.

"I ain't goin' home without it," I say. "They ain't gonna kill my boy without a fight. I'm gonna come back every day. I'm gonna sit out there on those steps every day until I see him."

These words coming out that I never thought of before.

"That's your prerogative," he say.

Whatever that means.

It's a free country, it means.

I walk out of that office without saying good-bye. And bump into some man going in. Out in the lobby the ceiling is very high. I noticed that before. Now I understand why. It makes folks who come feel small. Real small.

My armpits is sweating in my dress. My heart thumping from upset. I go outside. The white stone steps sweep down, toward the flowers smiling at the bottom. I hear my own words and sit on the steps to rest.

Across the street a group of ladies is walking, round and round in a circle. Holding up signs with writing on them and yelling things. And a truck nearby and a television camera on the ground, taking pictures. And a man holding a microphone talking to a lady. And the others in the background, waving their signs and yelling.

I walk down the steps to see what they yelling about. I read the words on their signs.

"Legal Abortion Is Legal Murder," they say.

And other things.

Leroy Briggs ➤ Cheater Charlie tell me where to

meet him. A bar on Gun Hill Road. Ten o'clock.

I leave the money at home. Cheater Charlie ain't called Cheater for nothin'.

The place is dark inside, till your eyes become accustom'. People at the bar is laughing, drinking beer. I pass by. Cheater at a booth in the back, by hisself.

Cheater nod his head. I slide in opposite.

Cheater drinking beer from a glass. The bartender come, wiping his hands on his apron, and stand nearby.

"What you drinkin'?" he says.

"A beer," I say.

The bartender look at Cheater.

"Bring him a Coke," Cheater say.

The bartender walk away.

"You pretty dumb, boy," Cheater say. "What are you, twelve years old?"

"Sixteen," I say.

"Same thing," Cheater say.

The bartender brings the Coke and waits. I give him a dollar. He doan bring no change.

I sip the Coke. Too sweet, it tastes. Enough to make you sick.

"Well," Cheater say. "What is it you want? I got appointments to keep."

I tell him what I want.

Cheater sip his beer. He look me hard in the face.

"What you want that for?" he say.

I look him back in the face, just as hard.

"My business," I say. "Not yours."

Cheater screw up his lips. Then he nod his head.

"Now you talkin' like a man," he say.

I say nothing. Though what he say makes me feel good. Cheater sips his beer.

"Could be provided," he says. "For the right price, of course."

Of course. He think I want it free?

"How much?" I say.

"Fifty," he say. "Fifty bucks."

Hot damn!

I pretend to think it over.

"Okay," I say after a time. "Sounds like a fair price."

Cheater sips his beer again. Hiding his expression. I can tell he is surprise' I have that much. He puts the beer down slow.

"Wait," he says. "I ain't finished. That's fifty bucks plus."

"Plus what?" I say, screwing up my eyes. Damn cheater. "Fifty is all I got."

"I didn't say money," he says.

"What then?"

Cheater winks.

"You know that piece of ass you got," he says.

I doan say nothing. My heartbeat start running away.

"You know the one I mean. What's her name?"

"Angel?" I say. My voice a little weak, and sick.

"That's the one," Cheater say. "Fifty bucks plus a little piece of ass."

I look him in the face.

"Jesus, Cheater, you can get all you want."

"Yup," Cheater say. "An' that's the one I want."

"Shit, no," I say. "No deal."

"Okay," Cheater say. And he slide out of the booth. "No deal."

He sip his last of beer standing up, ready to walk away. My head spinning around. Where else I got to go?

"Wait," I say. "I'll ask her."

Cheater smile down.

"Ain't no need," he say. "I'll bring what you need Tuesday

night. The parking lot out back. You have Angel there." He smile again. "Ain't no need to ask her."

The parking lot. Sheet.

"No parking lot," I say. "You come to my place. I got the whole place empty. A bed and everything."

Cheater wink again.

"Now you talkin', boy." Then he grab my chin in his hand and look hard in my face. "You wouldn't be thinkin' a messin' with old Cheater, would you?"

I shake my head. Feeling all weak inside.

"Good," he says. "We got us a fair deal."

Daralyn Kirk ➤ They took us to a carnival with silver cars all round in the sky and people screaming and others
all round on the ground. And other cars bumping and sticky
pink to eat which gets all over my face till I wipe it off with
my sleeve. My dress pink too so it won't show. And balloons
filled with water and basketball to shoot and rifles and stuffed
animals you can win only nobody from our place do. Only they
give us anyway. They give me a furry brown mouse and say
I win it, and everybody clap. I stick it in my purse. I didn't win
it.

There is a merry-go-round with red horses and green and
yellow. I want to get on a horse and ride away. They say I is
too big for the horses so I start to cry, and they let me.
Sometimes when you cry they let you. I get on a red horse and
it is not big enough like they say but I stay on anyway, round
and round. The horse saddle in me under my dress. Down
there. Making me wet, and the music go round and round, and
the horse and me. They don't let us men in the night. And
everyone laughing at big Daralyn on the little horse, round
and round. And me smiling too.

Then it is time to go and we is walking in the street to the
bus. And then I see him. Brown in his black jacket on his black
bike. The bike spitting noise at the curb. I run to him yelling,
hey, you, but he don't hear me. The bike run away a bit. Then
at the corner it stop at a red light, and me running after. I
want to go with him. Wherever. I run up breathing breath and
the noise from the bike. Hey, it's me, I say. Take me with you.
And him turn and look at me with his face all scrunched, like
he don't know who I am. It's me, I say, it's Daralyn, don't you

remember? Then the nurse grab me and pull me away from the greenlight honking cars. And the bike spurt out and away blowing noise. And him with it.

I want to go with him, I yell, pulling from the nurse. But the other nurse come and hold me tight. I try to cry again. This time they don't let me.

It wasn't him, they say. Him still away there in jail. I know it was him, I say. I saw his name on the bike.

Then I stop my crying. Maybe it wasn't him. If it was him he would've took me.

Walter Briggs ► I lay on my bunk and stare at the

ceiling, at the dark spot getting bigger as I stare. And think these thoughts I don't like to think. That come back more and more, like a cat someone's been feeding milk to. Or mice.

I think there is a difference between Jonesy and me. A difference that don't seem to make no difference. That he is guilty and I am innocent. How can a difference like that not make no difference? How can the way you lived your life not make no difference to what happens?

I think about why I was put here on earth. To die like this? It don't make sense. They say that Jesus died for our sins. If I die it will be for one person's sin, and no one knows who it is. What's the good of that?

I ask if there is a God. I don't know the answer. Those who believe there is say He works in mysterious ways. If there is one, He sure as shit do.

Sometimes I pray. I never prayed before except that time in Lake Jonah when my father went away. But I didn't pray about my father. I was in a rowboat on the lake with Leroy, and the sky got dark and thunder came up and lightning all around, and we were scared. I prayed that the lightning wouldn't hit us. And it didn't. "See," I said to Leroy, "my prayer was answered." "Mine wasn't," Leroy said. "What was yours?" I said. "That Daddy come home," he said. "The thing is," I told him, "God controls the lightning, but He don't control people." Some jive malarkey I made up.

Only now I think maybe it's true.

Sometimes I pray. If there is a God, maybe He will hear me.

If there is no God, I get tired of talking to Jonesy sometimes anyway.

The truth is, I don't believe it will happen. I don't believe it will happen to Jonesy on Monday. And he is guilty. I surely don't believe it will happen to me, who done nothing wrong. The Governor will stop it, like Miss Marshall is asking. Or the real killer will confess, to save me. So that I don't die. Somehow I will be saved. This hope and knowledge is what keeps me going from day to day.

Sometimes in despair I think the only way is to escape. Then I look down at my hands, and out at the bars, and the walls across the yard, and the guard towers on top with guns. And I know I can't, and I lie down in a sweat, and the dark spot on the ceiling gets bigger, so big it fills the ceiling and begins to creep down the walls.

It is no good to think of these things. It is better just to live day by day. I . . .

"Briggs!"

The nice guard is outside my cell, the one whose name I don't know. Not Jackson. I haven't seen Jackson for days.

"Yeah?"

He is opening my cell with his keys.

"Get yourself pretty," he says. "You're goin' to see the warden."

"The warden?"

My heart starts jumping in my chest. A balloon of air is filling my chest, getting bigger and bigger. In two years I ain't never seen the warden!

I look around for what I need to take. There is nothing I need to take.

"The warden? What for? What's it about?"

"Don't know," he says. "They just told me to bring you."

I look at his face, close. There's no expression one way or the other.

I go into the corridor. Jonesy is sitting on his bunk, looking at the floor.

"Hey, Jonesy," I say. "What do you think?"

Jonesy looks up, his eyes kind of sad, as if it is all getting to him now, and shrugs his shoulders. He flips the butt he is smoking into the john, a bull's-eye with a hissing sound. Then he looks back at the floor.

All the while the balloon in my chest is lifting me off the ground. The warden! It must have happened! They discovered their mistake at last! They are going to set me free! All this racing through my brain, and me trying not to show it. So as not to make Jonesy jealous. But I can't stop the racing thoughts as I walk down the hallways with the guard, past one gate, then another. I wonder with excitement how it happened. The Governor must've done it. I could kiss Miss Marshall all over. The Governor must've done it. Or maybe the killer got caught. Even better. Maybe the killer confessed or got caught.

Whatever, it don't matter. It's over, all over. I'm free. The warden wants to tell me the good news himself. I'm free!

We cross the yard. The warden's office is in a building behind two fences, at the other end. I look up at the sky. It is bluer than it's been in two years. So blue I want to cry. The balloon in my chest lifting me off the ground so I can hardly walk right. I'm almost skipping, like a kid.

Free at last. Just like it says in the song. Free at last.

Virgil LeFontaine ▶

Max is away on vacation. (Max Bloom—Flowers, the sign says. Joycean and medieval and the Marx Brothers all in one.) The clock shows two minutes to twelve. I am about to close for lunch when they tinkle through the door. Her eyes red from weeping above a slinky black dress. (Don't you just love those, under the circumstances? Black, but slinky?) His face a stoic mask. Sad but strong. To her a rock to lean on. To me he didn't give a damn. Is not altogether unhappy the poor bastard is dead. A tough one to figure. Her first husband, I'd guess. And this one on her arm has never been his match.

"We need to send flowers to a funeral," he says. "Could you recommend something appropriate?"

We need.

"White lilies are always in good taste," I say.

"How much are those?"

She starts to weep, quietly, and pulls a handkerchief from her bag.

"Eighteen dollars a dozen."

"Do you have anything chea . . ."

"We'll take the lilies," she manages to blurt through her tears. "Two dozen. Give him the address, George."

"Two dozen? But, hon, he's dea . . ."

She pokes his arm.

"Two dozen lilies," he says. He finds a card in the breast pocket of his blue suit. "Send them to this address."

The Forest Chapel, just two blocks away. She wanted to go to the funeral, and he forbade it. The flowers a compromise.

"How shall the card read?" I say. And wait expectantly.

131

"Elizab . . ." she begins.

"Mr. and Mrs. George Frazier," he says.

She sniffles back a new outburst of tears that would have been too threatening. While he pays, cash. Then they are gone, she a bit rickety on her high heels, and I put the "Closed" sign in the door.

For the moment I feel exhausted. A flower shop is no place for a sensitive person to work. People think otherwise, of course. Surrounded by blossoms all day. The roses, red and pink and yellow, the orchids, the carnations, a mixture of euphoric scents. But that is only the surface, the petal skin. Beneath it, moving like a snake through the ferns, the waxed paper, is the blood of life. A baby is born, some flowers for the new madonna. The old man dies, flowers for the grave. The cancer is terminal? Roses for the hospital room window. An orchid to help him get into her panties after the senior prom. A carnation at graduation. And the bride (knocked up on the baseball field two months before) wore a tulle veil and carried baby's breath. A single red rose for his mistress. Lilies to mourn his passing. The seven ages of man, soiling one's fingers each day. Life and death, illusion and sadness, leap-frogging through the mornings and afternoons into eternity. An emotional roller coaster, if you are at all aware.

I lock the door behind me, clutching the attaché case in the other hand, and walk to the corner, to the bus marked Desire. At the bank she is there as always in a flowered dress that can hardly contain her thighs. She tries to be pleasant, but I dispense with it. It has been a rough morning. We go through the ritual of the key. A primal rite between strangers. Until at last I am alone in the little room. I have not brought lunch. After rough mornings diversion is more nourishing than food.

I remove the new clipping from the case. I find the next page of the ledger, and with care I paste it in. A small one. It is the small ones that build up to the big one. This one says:

BRIGGS'S LAWYER
ASKS CLEMENCY
FROM GOVERNOR

I close the ledger and prepare to begin at the beginning.

But for the first time I am too fatigued. Is the whole subject beginning to bore me?

Mother's Day is the worst, by far. They come in droves. Roses for Mama. A nice begonia for Mama. A mixed bouquet. An orchid for her dress. A nice plant for the house. Mama Mama Mama. Sometimes we get lucky. Someone dies. Not one in ten, though. Not even one in a hundred. Mama Mama Mama. Till you want to retch.

It was then, that first Mother's Day, two years ago, that he appeared. Hidden among the flowers. And told me what I must do. Not here, he said, but far away, in a part of the country I had seen only in books. Amid the twisted mistakes of nature. In a sordid park of pagan images. In Utah.

("I need to go away," I told Max. "To visit my sick mama in Philadelphia.")

("Sure," he said, "go. Now that the rush is over.")

He was waiting in the park, as he had promised.

To guide me.

To choose.

("She's feeling much better. Yes.")

I was feeling much better myself.

I close the ledger, unread. For some reason tears come to my eyes. Weeping for Elizabeth's first love, whoever he was. Weeping for everyone's first love.

I soil my handkerchief, wiping away the tears. And force myself to sit in the small room for half an hour more. So she will not be able to see I have been crying.

Walter Briggs ➤ All these thoughts racing through

my head as we climb up the steps to the warden's office, me and the guard I don't know. Thoughts of freedom days. The blue sky and the water at Orchard Beach where Mama used to take us to swim on Sunday afternoons in summer, after she come home from church. Me and Leroy splashing around while Mama sat on the beach under a big umbrella, just enough room to walk on the hot sand between our blanket and the one alongside. Always some lady in curlers on the one alongside, reading movie magazines with a portable radio playing. And on the other side sometimes a man drinking beer with another radio playing the Mets if I was lucky, or the Yankees if he was a jerk. The man yelling at the lady to turn her radio down. The lady yelling at the man, "Screw you." Mama in the middle reading the *Daily News* as if she don't hear nothing. Over the whole crowded beach a hum of noise like flies. Eighty thousand people jammed Orchard Beach, the radio would say on extra-hot days, and the parking lots full and the tar melting sticky under your sneakers, only we had to take the bus, scrunched in. Mama buying us hot dogs and soda and saying to wait half an hour before we go back in. So as not to get cramps. I grab the rest of Leroy's soda and dance away. He comes running after, and I run into the water and splash away. We never waited half an hour. We never got cramps, neither. Maybe it happens when you're old. Another time splashing in the water throwing a Spaldeen back and forth and diving under for it I came face to face with a turd. A big brown turd that bumped into my nose. That somebody laid right there in the water. I splash away screaming in fake fright and real disgust. Leroy says, "What's the matter?" "Run, quick, run," I yell, "it's a man-eating turdfish." "What's that?" Leroy says. "It's bigger than a shark," I said. Leroy ran out of the water and wouldn't come back in all day. In college we read in freshman English that story about a bananafish. I don't know what he meant by bananafish, but turdfish they got plenty at Orchard Beach. "Why you scare your brother half to death like that?" Mama said. "'Cause he's got to learn not to be so scared," I said. Which is easy to say when you are small. Though Leroy did outgrow it pretty quick. That year he grew five inches and thickened out and started lifting weights.

"In here," the guard says, and opens a wooden door. A trusty is sitting at a desk, typing. He nods to me as we pass. I nod back. I don't know him.

We go through another door, past two secretaries with hair pulled tight, as if they was purposely trying not to look pretty. And then another office, the warden sitting behind a big wooden table with nothing on it except a folder that must be mine.

"This is Briggs, sir," the guard says.

The warden stands. Pointy darts jabbing at the balloon in my chest. Trying to break it. I think, he stood up for me. That is a good sign. Only free men get respect.

"Have a seat, Briggs," the warden says, and motions to a chair. I sit in the curved wooden chair, across the table from him.

"You can wait outside," he says to the guard. The guard goes out and closes the door behind him. My eyes leap automatic to the windows. There are bars on the windows, even in the warden's office. The jailers and the jailed all together. But it's no more matter to me, I tell myself. In a few more minutes I will be free.

The warden sits and leans back in his chair and pulls out a pack of cigarettes and lights one.

"Smoke?" he says to me, holding out the pack.

I tried it once when I was twelve and coughed my head off. I never smoked since. I shake my head.

"Good," he says, blowing smoke and putting the pack

away. "I'm gonna quit myself one of these days."

I listen to what he is saying and say nothing. From a street outside I can hear horns honking, traffic moving. You can't hear none of that from the cell.

"How are they treating you?" the warden says.

"Okay," I say. Wishing he would get on with it. My hands sweating, my muscles all tight. Like the first few times with Mrs. Hawthorne. Till I loosened up.

"You getting enough food, enough exercise?"

I nod my head. One hand squeezing the other wrist in my lap under the table where he can't see. Why don't he get on with it?

He seems to read my thoughts. He leans forward and opens the folder on the table. There's something about the way he does that. Some weariness. The darts break the balloon in my chest. All my muscles sag. If I wasn't sitting I would have fallen down.

"I suppose you know why you're here," he says.

My head shakes no, then yes, then no again. I'm all mixed up. My head spinning around. A feeling I felt once before, but I can't place when. Then it hits me what he is doing, just as he begins to talk. He doesn't even talk. He reads it from a card in the folder.

Choose!

"Having been duly convicted . . ."

Choose!

"The morning of July 14, 19 . . ."

Choose!

The one word ringing like a gong inside my head. My head spinning like I now remember when. When I seen the referee waving his arms that it was too late. That it don't count. The crowd yelling boos then like the word screams now in my head.

Choose!

"Death by hanging, or death by firing squad, the option to be that of the prisoner's. Walter Briggs, as warden of the state penitentiary it is therefore my duty now to ask you . . ."

The words passing by like wind that you cannot see. Wind

136

that ripples your hair and moves on. Wind that is the engine of sailboats.

I have never ridden in a sailboat.

"I'll ask you again, Walter. Which do you choose?"

Like some terrible dream from which I will soon awake.

I come out of it. I look at the warden's face. It is serious but kindly. Like a professor at a college.

He is sitting there, waiting. From somewhere he has gotten an ashtray. He crushes out the cigarette. Bible words break apart in my head. Ashes . . .

I refuse to hear them. I say nothing. I wait for him to speak again. As if I am in some play, waiting to hear what part we are up to.

Josephine Briggs ➤ The ladies walking round and round with their signs. Personally I ain't never had much use for signs. Signs say, This I Believe, or they say, You Stink. But they don't say the whys and the wherefores. Life is made up mostly of whys and wherefores.

Still, oftentimes you got to do what you don't like to do. Life is made up mostly of that, too.

I find a store a few blocks away that's got big white cardboard and Crayola crayons. The crayons remind me of a little girl. They was the only toy she had, and she used to draw and draw all day. She was a real good drawer. Everybody said she would be a famous artist someday. I take the cardboard and the crayons to a little park across the street and sit on a bench and write the sign. Black and green I choose. It seems the best. Though as a chile my favorite was red. I put the crayons in my purse and I carry the sign in my hand, facing in, and I walk back. The ladies still is walking round and round. But the television truck is gone. I walk up the steps and I sit on the ground where I was before, holding the sign up beside me. Like an artist displaying her work.

A whole hour I must've sat there, my backside aching from the steps. Wanting to stretch real bad, but don't. People pass by and they look at my sign, and then they look at me. Like I am crazy. And then they walk on, whispering together. I start to think it was a dumb idea. The Governor might not come this way at all.

Then another truck comes. Another truck from a TV station, and begin to take pictures of the abortion ladies walking round and round. And talk to some of them, holding a microphone. Then one of the men with a camera point to me, sitting with my sign. And they come and take my picture. And the man with the microphone ask me what it is about, and I tell him, and he asks if he can ask me some questions with the camera on, and I say shoot. So he asks me with the microphone by my chin what my sign means, "Please Don't Kill My Boy." And I tell him my Walter is a good boy who ain't never been in trouble and wouldn't do nothing like that, and they is going to kill him in two weeks unless the Governor say no. It's all a mistake, I say. And that I come out by bus from the Bronx to ask the Governor to say no. Only the Governor too busy to see me, so I make a sign. All this I tell him with the camera on me and my sign, and after he thanks me very much. A nice young man, he was. "This gonna be on the TV?" I say. "The six o'clock news," he says. "You think the Governor watches that?" I say. "I don't know," he says, "but I'm sure he'll hear about it."

When the truck pulls away I keep sitting there with my sign. The abortion ladies packing up to go home. Some of them giving me a dirty look. Josephine Larner Briggs, I says to myself, maybe you ain't so dumb as you like to think.

Walter Briggs ▶ Jonesy stands up and grips the

bars when we get back. I can see his knuckles white. I go into the cell. The guard I don't know locks it behind me and goes away. I hear Jonesy scratching a match against the wall. I hear him puffing, and breathing. I hear him about to speak before he speaks.

"What'd you choose?" he says.

I turn around and stare across the way into his eyes.

"How'd you know?" I say.

"What else could it be?" he says.

Yeah. What else could it be?

I turn and cross the cell and look out the high window into the yard. Shit, it ain't Jonesy's fault. I turn and go back again. He's standing there smoking by the bars.

"I didn't," I say.

He looks at me, dumblike.

"You didn't choose?"

I look down at the floor. Some kind of embarrassment creeping over. Like when you are called on to speak in class. I was always embarrassed to speak in class. For no reason.

"I figure it's a trick," I say. "Why else would they make you choose? Why not do everyone the same? This way they get you to confess. You choose, do it this way, do it that way, it's like saying okay, I'm guilty, do what you got to do. It's like giving them permission. I figure, shit, I ain't gonna give them no blessing."

"You figured it good, kid," Jonesy says.

That's what I figured. I figured it good. Especially with that appeal still out.

"The only thing," Jonesy says, "that gives them the choice."

"Yeah," I say.

Jonesy blows smoke across.

"Well, speak up," he says. "What'd the warden choose?"

I look back across. He is like a dark outline now, the bulb in his cell behind him. Like a cardboard cutout, talking.

"Firing squad," I say.

Jonesy nods and puffs again.

"At least he gave you a break," he says.

I'm not sure if he is joking or serious. With Jonesy you never can tell. Then I think of one of his jokes. I start to say it.

Jonesy says the exact same thing, at the exact same time.

"They're all heart."

We look at each other's dark face.

Then we laugh.

Josephine Briggs ➤ I sit on the steps till the building empties out. I don't see the Governor nohow. There's lots of side doors all over. I take my sign after the crowd passes and go home on the bus to "Transients." I put it in the room and eat spaghetti in the bus depot down the street and go on back to the room. I take off my dress and hang it neat, though the backside is awful wrinkled, and put on my old pink robe. I take down the Bible but get another idea. I open the drawer in the little table and sure enough there is paper there and postcards with pictures of the hotel on it when it was new. The postcards and the paper old yellow as if nobody has used them since. As if people who come to "Transients" don't write. First I write a postcard to Leroy with the ball pen I brought in my purse:

> Dear Leroy, I hope to see Walter on Sunday. I hope to bring him home soon. Be a good boy don't make trouble for Cora. Love Mama.

I leave the postcard on the side to mail in the morning, and I take some of the papers from the drawer. And get the crayons from my purse and start to draw pictures on the papers, pretty pictures with all the colors of the rainbow. Lordy, I ain't done nothing like that since I was twelve. I was so caught up I didn't see the time till it was dark. I clean forgot all about the news. It didn't much matter, though. There ain't no TV in "Transients," and I was too dog-tired to go out. Instead I looked at the pictures I drew for a while. Smiling and pleased. Then I threw them in the trash and went to bed. The fire light blinking on the walls.

142

In the morning I put on my white blouse and my old blue skirt with the hem I fixed and carry my sign rolled up and take the whichnumber bus back up to the capitol. And sit in the same place on the steps again. Not knowing if it will do any good, but I can't go see Walter till Sunday. It being Saturday there are less people going in and out and the abortion ladies aren't there. But after a time a TV truck come anyway. They want to talk to me. "I talk to you yesterday," I say. "That was another station," he say. And I hold up my sign and I tell him again about Walter. Then they get a man out from inside. It is the same man I saw in his office. They ask him questions about why the Governor won't see Mrs. Briggs. I stand to the side and listen as he answers.

"The Governor has received an appeal for clemency from the attorney in the case. He is studying that appeal and will reach a decision on the merits of the case. To see Mrs. Briggs, for whom the Governor has the utmost sympathy, would merely inject unnecessary emotionalism into the issue."

The TV men thank him and he goes back inside. I run through my head what he said. That they want to kill my boy without no emotions. I think, people got strange notions in this world.

The TV truck goes away. Most of the steps is empty. I go on back to my place and sit with my sign. There ain't nothing better to do that I can think of. I want to go see that lady lawyer but will do that Monday, after I talk to Walter. The sun is hotter and sweat is on my face. I wipe it with a handkerchief from my purse. Sometimes just doing nothing is the hottest thing of all. All the time I keep glancing at a lady standing near a pillar off to one side. Like she was waiting for the TV people to leave. And waiting longer till they are far away and no more people around. Then she walks over, slow-like, carrying cardboard of her own. She has gray hair done neat and is wearing a plain brown dress with a gold buckle. And nice stockings and shoes. She looks down at me as if she don't know what to say. Then she says, "May I sit beside you?" "It's a free country," I say, and she sits on the steps beside me. Careful-like, like she is not used to sitting on steps. Though I ain't neither.

143

"You're Mrs. Briggs," she says.

"That's right," I say.

"I saw you on television last night."

Then it was!

"I think your cause is just," she says. "I think Walter is innocent."

I look at her. It feels good.

"You know my Walter?" I say.

"No," she says. "But I've followed the case closely."

I nod my head. I don't know exactly what to say.

"Do you mind if I display a sign also?" she says.

I shrug my shoulders. Why should I mind?

She turns over the white cardboard she has got. The letters are big in dark blue paint. Arranged like this:

WALTER
BRIGGS
IS
INNOCENT

I look at the sign, and I look at her, and tears come to my eyes. They come to my eyes and they run all down my cheeks. I don't go to wipe them because more is coming down. More and more. And I don't be ashamed. I reach my arm around and hug that lady I don't know. I hug her shoulder to my shoulder. At first she holds back a bit, like she is the kind of person who don't like to be hugged. Then she lets go her sign and hugs me all around. Tears running down both faces. Crying with this lady I never saw before, and neither of us paying no mind. Just crying.

After a time we pulls away and wipes our faces. Sniffling and smiling at each other through the tears. Then we sit side by side, holding up our signs for anyone to see who passes by.

Belinda Marshall ➤ Saturday afternoon in the capitol press room. Nobody here but me. Four battered wooden desks, old Underwood typewriters. Filing cabinets stuffed with yellowed clippings. Scrapbooks of the public side of life. The faint odor of old copy paper. Gray light behind windows opaque with grime. Somewhere in the building a cleaning lady working her way this way.

Maybe she'll scrub my soul.

I haven't gone out since Eric. After two years you're out of circulation. Not that I've wanted to. My opinion of men is not at its peak right now. My flesh crawls, I feel myself shaking inside, every time I think of him.

Last night I ate cottage cheese and fruit salad. Keeping the old ass firm for the next one. Why are we slaves to these others? And curled up alone and watched TV, a grand old movie on cable I always wanted to see. *I Am a Fugitive from a Chain Gang.* Paul Muni marvelous. They don't make movies like they used to. (Brilliant, Belly, brilliant.) But it's true. They don't . Nothing but earthquakes and disasters. Nothing with a point of view, nothing with real people. They can say fuck all they want to on the screen. But intelligence is a dirty word. Makes you wonder about our society.

(Thank you, Judge Marshall.)

After the film the news came on. The President, the Middle East. I was half paying attention when suddenly they were talking about Walter. Talking to a woman on the steps of the capitol. His mother. Speaking bravely, holding a sign.

Street-smarts, in Utah? Could it work?

My feeling was no. He's a stranger here, always has been.

145

There is little sleep lost in Salt Lake City over Walter Briggs.

Still, I wanted to meet her.

I had to work this morning. Usually I wear jeans on Saturday with court not in session, but I figured a dress would give her more confidence. After lunch I called the press room. She had come back, all right. She was still out there. I drove on over.

There weren't many people about as I climbed the mall. The profusion of flowers testifying to the beauty of life, even if sometimes I wonder, steeped in the seamy side. I've often thought a simple workaday life would be nice. Without causes. Waitress in a diner. Clerk in a flower shop. Something like that.

I was surprised to see two of them as I climbed the steps. Walter's mother and a white woman beside her. Both of them holding signs.

"Mrs. Briggs?" I said.

"Yes?"

"I'm Belinda Marshall. Walter's attorney."

Her face brightened as if I were the Second Coming. She put her sign down and stood, smoothing her skirt, or wiping her hand on it, or both, and shook my hand.

"I'm so pleased to meet you. I was going to call."

She turned. The other woman had remained seated on the steps. Reluctantly she stood to be introduced.

"Miss Marshall, this is my friend, Miss Sarah."

We shook hands. As I looked at her my jaw went slack, my hand limp.

"Yes, I . . ."

She was slightly behind Mrs. Briggs. She was shaking her head from side to side, faintly, an imploring look in her eyes.

"I'm pleased to meet you," I said.

We talked for several minutes. I told Mrs. Briggs to give my best to Walter the next day. When I asked where she was staying, so I could keep in touch, she hesitated, seeming embarrassed. Mrs. Merton spoke for her.

"Mrs. Briggs was staying at a hotel. But they're so expensive these days and not very comfortable. I've prevailed on her to stay with me for a while."

I was speechless. Portia with mud in her mouth.

"I have my own apartment now," Mrs. Merton said. "It's not very far from here, and there's a fold-down bed in the living room. Mrs. Briggs will be staying there."

I nodded, no words coming.

"Would you like the telephone number?"

"Yes, of course."

Trying not to look as flustered as I was. And found a pad in my purse. She wrote it down.

To Mrs. Briggs I said, "Will you be sitting outside here with your sign every day?"

It was Mrs. Merton who replied. "Yes. We'll be sitting here together."

The rest is a blur. They asked me if I thought it would help. I told them I didn't know; that it couldn't hurt. Then I left them and fled inside, into the dim brown cave of deserted lobby, and sank onto a bench. My head was in a whirl. I was trying to calculate the reaction and finding it impossible to predict.

I can't do it, I told myself. But the legs that Eric loved to love carried me to the press room. Jim Barnes of the *Tribune* was still here.

We made idle chatter for a time. I knew him some from his courthouse days. My mongoose brain seeking the right words.

"You do anything about Mrs. Briggs and her sign?" I said.

"A short feature for tomorrow," Barnes said. "Are you behind it?"

"I didn't even know she was coming. Scout's honor. It was her own idea."

"That's what she said."

"By the way," I added, trying to fight the melodrama, "who's the lady sitting with her?"

"What lady?"

"Some white woman. Local. Has a sign saying Walter Briggs is innocent. She seems to have joined Mrs. Briggs for the duration."

"Don't know," Barnes said.

He let the subject drop. I reached back for a reserve.

"Could be a nice twist," I said. "Local white woman joins New York black lady's cause. Fights to save her son. I wonder who she is. What her own family will think."

Barnes had been leaning on the back two legs of his chair. He let the chair fall forward.

"You're too smart to be telling me how to do my job," he said.

"I wouldn't do that. Would I?"

He cocked his head and peered at my face.

"Well, out with it," he said. "What the hell *are* you trying to tell me?"

I picked up a newspaper from a nearby desk and looked at the front page.

"Me?" I said. "I'm not even here."

He gave me one long puzzled look, grabbed a pad and his jacket, and hurried out the door.

Triumph!

An exultant feeling in my heart.

A coat of tarnish on my soul.

Welcome to the world of the creeps and the sellouts, Belly Marshall.

But it's a good cause, I tell myself.

Yes, I answer myself, it always is.

Barnes comes rushing in a few minutes later. He blows me a kiss as he passes, and grabs the phone on his desk. He asks for photo, and then the city desk. As he waits he cups his hand over the phone.

"You doing anything for dinner tonight?" he says.

What the fuck, Belly. It was only a matter of time. Someone would have recognized her, sooner or later.

I try not to bat my eyes. (One does get out of practice.) A faint modicum of pleasure in my voice.

Which I am surprised to discover is genuine.

"As a matter of fact, I happen to be free."

Daralyn Kirk ➤ The man what sweeps the halls with a big fat broom comes in my room which is open and closes the door behind. And says he has a letter from him. A letter for me from him. Well give it me, I say. But first he say I got to do something first. Oh yeah, I say, you ain't got no letter from him. You show me a letter from him. He pull out his pocket and inside a letter from him. He holds it and I look at it close. I know it is true it from him.

You give it me, I say, it has its thirteen cents. Special delivery, he say, laughing with broken teeth. You got to do what I say. Oh yeah, I say, I'll go and tell that nurse. Oh yeah, he say, who you think give me that letter? Oh yeah, I say, why would she do that? Oh yeah, he say, I give her five dollars for it. So you just go and tell.

When we finish he give me the letter and take his broom and go. I pull it open excited and read it all. All writ in blue ink on paper. He still there in jail, he say, and glad to get my letter and sorry he not writ before. He don't think they will let me come visit him in jail and bring a gun. I shouldn't be sorry all the time about what I said. They would've lock him up any way, he said. They twisted my words all around it wasn't my fault. I just got to keep saying the truth now, he said, the way I said to my friend Michael Maller when he writ it in that newspaper that time. Make sure I keep saying the truth from now, he said, but not to worry always it weren't my fault. He wish he could visit me too, he said, but they don't let him out neither. He like me a lot like I thought 'cause at the top he wrote dear Daralyn and everything. Dear Daralyn. Though at the bottom he wrote Walter Briggs which was not his name

149

then, I think. Maybe he change it in jail. Maybe he not want his mama and stuff to know.

I fold the letter and put it in the pocket of my dress. Then I sit on my chair and pull it out and read it all again. Dear Daralyn. Then I fold it up and put it in the pocket of my dress. Then I lay on my bed and take it out and hold it up and read it all again.

Again and again I read it all till it is time for lunch. Then I hide it in my slipper under the bed, so nobody will come and steal it. The way they do.

Simon W. Merton ► Damn!

Damn damn damn damn damn.

I'm looking at her picture, and still I don't believe it. The goddamned blasted front page! Of the Sunday paper, no less. If she walked in right now, I could kill her. I swear it. Just thinking about what court will be like tomorrow, I could kill her with my bare hands.

The nerve! The goddamned nerve! Why didn't she just come and cut my balls off with her garden shears?

Thirty years! You live with a person thirty years, and you don't see the hatred building up. The odorless, tasteless, invisible, poisonous hatred. Of the Lawfully Wedded Spouse.

There's a question they should ask Walter Briggs. What in hell's so bad about dying young?

151

Josephine Briggs ➤ Miss Sarah's place is nice. The furniture is furnished, she said, because she just went away from her husband, but it is neat and clean with carpeting and drapes. And out the window a view of the mountains inky black in the night.

She roasted a chicken for dinner, and lettuce and tomatoes beside. I wanted to help but she said no, to sit. I said I can't stay here no longer unless she let me help. Then she said okay. From now on we cook dinner together and do the dishes too. For as long as I want to stay. I start to say what about money but then I stop. I know she won't take it nohow anyway.

Later we sit in the living room and talk. She ask about my life, and I tell her childhood things, memories from Georgia long ago. The good things more than the bad. Which is mostly what you remember anyway, for which I thank the Lord. All the time we talk Miss Sarah is doing knitting. Making nothing that I can tell. Just a long black thing that curls off of her chair and piles high on the floor. For a long time I don't ask her what it is. Then I can't help myself. It don't be anything, she says. Just knitting.

I shrug my shoulders without shrugging them. She is as nice a lady as I have met. If she like to knit like that, so what?

She take it inside the bedroom with her to sleep. In the morning we go to church around the block. And pray for Walter. Sitting alone together in the back, in a church she never been to before. After, we eat lunch in a coffee shop that is open. Tuna on toast for both. I ask her to tell about her life. There is not much to tell, she says. Most all her life at home in the state of Utah. Except when she went on some business trips with her husband. What does your husband do, I said, or did? He's with the government, she said.

I paid the both checks for the lunch. At first she wouldn't let me but she did. Then we went to where her car was parked, which her having one was the luckiest thing of all. And she drove me twenty miles to see my son.

Miss Sarah stayed in the car in the parking lot. You got to be alone with him, she said. It's only right. I go through different entrances and the guard check my package and my bag. What's in the package, he said. Candy bars, I said. Open it up, he said. It's all wrapped nice, I said. Sorry, he said, I got to open it. And he open up the wrapping and there it is. A six-pack like beer of six Snickers bars. Walter's favorite candy as a chile, and I know he like them still. The last thing his daddy ever bought him, that time on the bus.

Okay, the guard says, you can go. I try to wrap it again, but the tape don't stick too good. I hold it together with my hand. Inside more doors with bars, me trying not to look side to side. Till another guard open a room and let me in. Picnic tables all along. A wire fence in between. People and children visiting with prisoners on the other side. On this side of the fence just two picnic tables. Both empty.

"What's that side of the fence?" I ask the guard.

"General population," he says.

He don't say what this side is. I don't ask.

The guard goes out and I sit there alone. My hands smoothing the wrapping. My heartbeat fluttering away. As if trying to escape my chest, like a man locked in this place.

Two years I ain't seen my boy. Two years.

Then a door open on the other side of the room. A guard step aside. And Walter step in. The guard closing the door barely noticed behind him. All I can see is Walter, standing there. As if he don't want to come no closer.

I stand up near the table. I bite my lip to stop the tears from coming.

"Hello, Ma," Walter say.

"Hello, Son," I say.

Then he come closer, and I hug him around. My tears running down now, no matter what. Running down my cheeks

153

and on his shirt. His strong arms hugging me back. His face isn't crying, but inside I know he is.

I wipe my eyes and we sit at the table and talk. About how they is treating him, which is fine, he says. About if he gets enough to eat, which he does, he says. He ask about Leroy, who is fine, I say, and Cora and everyone. I ask what he does each day. He plays some basketball, he says, and talks to a friend of his. Tell me about your friend, I say. What you got in that package, he say. I give it to him. A little present, I say, and he opens it up. His favorite. He smiles like he did as a boy. Only not the same.

I take his hand on the table and hold it in mine. He leave it there but I see he isn't happy. Glancing at the others down the room, behind the wire fence. I guess he be too old now to have his mother hold his hand. Even there. I let it go.

We talk some more. He is there and not there at the same time. I don't remember what we talked about. Except that the guard said the half hour was up, and we hadn't said a thing. Nothing at all that mattered. As if there was things a human being shouldn't talk about. As if we were made of tinkly glass and all would come crashing down if we said the wrong word.

The guard said again it's time to go. I stood up from the table, and Walter too.

"Now don't you worry," I said. "You'll be out of this place soon. Won't be long before you walk out of here a free man. You'll see."

"I know, Mama," he said. "I know I will."

Simple and calm he said it. I know I will. Then the guard took me out and left him behind.

My knees was shaking till I found that car in the lot. And fell inside it on the seat. And cried and cried and cried and couldn't stop, Miss Sarah hugging me around. I cried till my throat was choking with the hurt. Till everything inside was emptied out. Then I wiped my face and sat up straight. And then I knew I wouldn't cry again, no matter what.

Walter Briggs ➤ It was like she wasn't there or I

wasn't there. She came but she wasn't my mother any more. Not like when you're little. To nourish and protect. A woman, a person, like any other, dwarfed by these walls, these bars. By the enormity. When they put you in a place where she cannot help you then you are still her son but she is not your mother any more.

Two years and there is nothing to talk about. Two years in this place and you feel ashamed. Even if you did nothing wrong, you feel ashamed. As if they know something about you that you yourself don't know. Some awful secret. Else why would you be here?

I couldn't even look at her. As if I was guilty. As if I had done what they said.

She came and I feel like shit. Worse than before. I try to see why, and I am ashamed. Because deep down she was my hope. Deep down there is always Mama, to fly in like a fairy and save you. But all there was was a tall black lady in a dress. And tears in her eyes. And nothing she can do.

And no more hope.

There was nothing to say. Not me to her nor her to me. Two years and you are like one of them children raised in the forest by wolves. You cannot speak to another.

The black stain looks down from the ceiling and smiles. They just give Jonesy his last meal. Steak and French fries and strawberry shortcake. He wolfed it down like he would never eat again.

I couldn't eat my food. Just some candy bar. And throwed it up, with the room spinning all around.

155

Simon W. Merton ➤ I packed the car last night and left at dawn, a thermos of hot coffee at my side. The brisk, silent city an empty gray. Escaping before it awakened. The first rays of the sun knifing over the mountains just as I reached the highway. Flaring in the windshield like a searchlight.

The cows on the farms outside of town already finished with milking when I passed.

McBride was understanding. Baker would cover for me. Postpone all my cases two weeks till I got back. The prudent thing to do, in the circumstances. (We would have been basking on the beach in Hawaii next week if Sarah hadn't left.)

I tried to think of the trout, hungry in Colorado. Instead I thought of prisons. Not those we build for criminals, but those we build for ourselves. The glass cocoons we spin around us with each passing year. Walling out spouses, acquaintances, friends. Walling in a desperate solitude. Born innocent, we nonetheless find ourselves guilty, and await with trepidation the unjust sentence of death we cannot escape. Appearing free, each to each, we are prematurely entombed. The static music of our lives the ticking of the clock.

Masochists anguish in empty rooms and listen to the ticking.

Others go to the movies. Or climb mountains.

Or go fishing.

Walter Briggs

➤ All night I lay awake, afraid to move. My eyes shut. The blanket pulled tight to my shoulder, to keep off the dripping of the black.

I want to talk to Jonesy, but I hear him breathing even. Sleeping like a baby.

I lay awake and don't move in the bed.

The longest night ever. A night of ghosts and witches. And cat eyes.

Black becomes gray in the cell. I am sweating beneath the blanket, as if I have a fever. I don't move.

There is shuffling in the corridor, shuffling in Jonesy's cell. I don't move.

The light opening from the window high in the wall like a magnifying glass.

Voices in Jonesy's cell. A guard, Jonesy, another. A minister. He didn't want one, but they sent one anyway. In case he changed his mind.

Voices talking.

"As long as you don't pray," Jonesy says.

The cell door opening, voices moving closer, into the corridor. My pajamas soaked with sweat, the blanket pulled tight. I don't move.

"Hey, Briggs."

Jonesy calling. I don't move. I know I should, but I don't.

"Hey, Briggs. I want to say good-bye."

I got to move. I don't want to, but I do. I push back the blanket and manage to stand. The floor is ice-cold. My slippers nowhere. Barefoot I stumble forward.

"Morning, champ," he says.

And smiles.

"Morning," I say.

He looks at my face. I look back at his.

He shoves out his arm. I stick my hand through the bars. We shake.

"Well, take it easy," he says.

"Yeah," I say. "You take it easy too."

He nods his head and winks.

The guard motions with his hand, down the corridor. Jonesy nods and turns and moves away. The guard and the minister behind.

The light coming brighter through the window high in the wall, that looks out on the yard. Like a magnifying glass.

I go back to my bunk and crawl in. And pull the blanket up tight, shivering against the cold.

I lay still. My eyes shut tight.

There is shuffling in the yard. Voices. I don't move.

The passage of time which is trying to rip me from the bed, toward the window. I hold tight to the sides of the bed with all my strength. And don't move.

It is as if time has stopped. And with it my breath.

In a minute I hear more voices.

Then a shout.

Then the explosion. One and then its echo playing volleyball across the yard. Drifting finally in through the window like a dying bird.

My body, taut and racked, goes limp against the mattress. My pajamas wet now with urine as well as sweat.

I don't move.

The light ever brighter through the window, like a magnifying glass. Brighter when it should be dimmer. When it should be going out.

The day is just beginning.

How can that be? That a day that begins like this goes on? With the sound of voices in the yard.

And then, at last, silence.

I don't move for a time. Then I push back the blanket. And

stand on the cold floor. And go to the window. As if a gun is leveled at my head. I lean up and peer out. The yard is empty, except for a trusty with a hose. Hosing down a place against the wall.

Daralyn Kirk ➤ The man with the great big broom ain't got no more. I ask him for another letter and he says he ain't got none. He says that I am crazy. I don't like it when people says things like that. The ones is crazy is going to kill Walter.

I like his new name better. Walter Briggs. When we is married it will be my new name too. Mrs. Walter Daralyn Briggs.

The man with the broom says there ain't gonna be no letters, that they will kill him soon. Then I get my plan. I will get a gun like I wrote in my letter and take it there and then I will get him free. Then I get my plan. You want more of what I do, I say to the man. There ain't no letters, he says. I don't care that, I say, I just like to do it to you all over. The man smile all over and say he would like that fine. But not in here, I say, with them nurses come along. Then where, he say, which is what I want him to say. Outside on the grass at night, I say. It's better on the grass all tickly. He smile again all over and got that look. That look that men get. But how you get outside, he say. At night they lock the doors. Tonight you leave that side door open, I say. Down by the end. Then when all asleep I tippytoe out and do it to you on the grass. It be real fun, I say. He smile and say it will. What time you come, he say. Eleven, I say. Eleven o'clock I come. After the lights is out and they asleep. You sure you'll come, he say. I'm sure I'll come, I say. If'n the door is open.

He go and I wait all day. And at night I take my dollars from my drawer and put it in the pocket of my dress. And lay down to sleep but don't sleep, till all the lights go out and it is quiet. Like that mouse they give me. And then I open the door slow and go out quiet in the hall past all the doors and no one around and come to that other and push it open and sure enough it is open. And then I am out in the dark with the grass feeling wet on my feet. And he is not there. And I smile, 'cause I knew he wouldn't be. 'Cause it is only ten o'clock. And I cross the grass in the dark and come to that fence. And climb up over which isn't hard except at the top there is points and when I jump down from the top on the other side the point catches my dress and rips it across. Rips it so one part hanging loose. I don't care. I run away from the fence and down the street in the dark. Staying by the walls that has no lights.

Leroy Briggs ► He came with somebody else. I
thought he would come alone and I could talk him out of it.
But he brought somebody else. A big bruiser, name of
Bruiser.

Angel was over and we was sitting on the sofa, watching
TV. The TV rolling around.

"Why don't you get that TV fixed?" Angel says.

"Ain't got no money," I say.

Angel thinks I'm some kind of millionaire.

"It's dumb watching TV like this," Angel says. "Let's go
inside and do it."

"A little while," I say. "I got this guy coming over, bringing
me something. After he leaves we can do it."

"What's he bringing you?" Angel says.

"Something."

Angel shrugs. We sit and watch TV. The black bar cutting
off heads. Till the doorbell rings and I go to answer it. Cheater
Charlie standing in the hall, holding this long white box. Behind him some three-hundred-pound guy.

"Flowers for Angel," Cheater says.

"Huh."

"She here?"

He steps inside and shoves the long white box in my hands.
It's heavy, not like flowers, and I almost drop it.

"Some flowers," I say.

"What you ordered," he says. "You got the money?"

I give him the fifty dollars from my pocket. Then I step back
toward the door, hoping they will leave. The three-hundred-
pound guy blocks open the door instead.

"Who's that?" I say to Cheater Charlie.

"Bruiser," Cheater says.

Cheater flashes white teeth from his jet-black face.

"Bruiser likes Angel too."

"No way," I say. "That ain't part of no bargain."

"We'll leave that up to Angel," Cheater says.

"Anyways, Angel ain't here," I say. "Angel's sick. You got to come back tomorrow."

"Oh yeah," Cheater says.

"Yeah."

Just then Angel calls out from inside.

"Hey, Leroy. What's takin' you so long?"

Dumb girl.

Not that they believed me anyways.

I'm still holding the box. I know it ain't loaded. Cheater wouldn't be that dumb.

"Wait here," I say to them.

And go down the hall to my room. I see them go into the living room. I hear them saying hello. And slip across to the bathroom and stick it in the hamper. Empty since Mama gone.

I come back to the living room. Angel not sure what's happening.

"Listen," I say.

"Beat it," Cheater says. "Go to the movies."

He reaches out to touch Angel's hair. Angel backs away down the sofa.

"Leroy, what's goin' on?" she says. Her eyes getting wide open with fright.

"I don't know," I say. "These guys are crazy."

Bruiser pulls a monkey wrench from his back pocket. He starts coming toward me, real slow. I start backing away, real slow. Till I am in the foyer and run out the door. And he closes it behind me, and I hear the lock turn.

I stand there in the hall, shaking. Not knowing what to do. Then I hear Angel scream. Scream again. I run down the stairs and out the door.

I walk through the streets without looking where. Then I am sitting in a movie, but I don't remember paying. On the screen is a ship that is sunk, upside down. With a lot of people

163

on it. All of them trying to get out, with the water rushing in. And them got to climb down to get up, 'cause the ship is upside down. And getting all mixed up, the whole world topsy-turvy. Not knowing the right thing to do. Not knowing how to get out. And drowning one by one as the water rises. The good along with the bad. And you don't know who'll be left at the end.

I leave before the end. What does it matter who's alive at the end?

I walk from dark to dark along Gun Hill Road. A little calmer now. It must be over by now. I pass the poolroom and think of going in. I look inside the door. Yellow circles of light, and guys bending over, and the clatter of the balls. Bumping one against another against another. Like with that guy kill some guy two years ago in Utah. And one thing bump against another. Bump and bump. And Cheater's ball landing in Angel's pocket. One bump leading to the next, and no one able to stop it.

I turn from the yellow circles and go on home. Walking slow. Making sure that it is over.

When I go upstairs the door is left wide open. I'm praying they didn't hurt her.

"Angel?"

I don't hear no answer.

"Angel, you here?"

No answer.

I go on inside. Into the living room. The lights still on, and the TV rolling with nobody watching it. Into my room. Everything ripped from the closet onto the floor. They was looking to take it back. Just like I knew. The whole room a mess.

I go across to the bathroom and open the hamper. It's still there, not touched. I leave it. For now.

I go into Mama's room. The bed all mussed. On the floor by the dresser Angel's white lace panties. Ripped almost to half.

Daralyn Kirk ➤ I run and run till my breath goes away and then I stop and walk. Always on streets in the dark. Till the street open up a world and there is the beach, the sand all soft underneath and a yellow white piece of moon looking down.

I walk along by the sea where the sand is wet and hard. Looking out to the sea. Somewhere across the sea is where he is. Across the sea is Utah and I don't know how to go.

I walk and walk and still it has no end. I come to shadows lying on the beach. 'Scuse me, I say, could you tell me which way to Utah. The both faces turn toward me. Beat it, the top one says. Get lost, the bottom one says. I scared and run away, 'cause both of them is men. Why he say get lost when I already?

I run and then I walk and then I sit. The sand all wet on my seat. Daralyn you got to be smart, I say, and pull the seven dollars from my dress. You gonna buy a gun with the money and have no money to go to Utah with. You gonna go to Utah with the money you gonna have no money to get a gun with. Daralyn, you got to be smart.

Only I ain't.

I put the money in my dress and stretch my side all sleepy in the sand. First I get some sleep and not be tired. Then I will be smart.

Virgil LeFontaine ➤ One of the old jazzmen has died. The funeral procession is wending its way beneath my window. The sweating men in their black suits and black bowlers or white admiral caps with black peaks, blowing and pounding a joyous rhythm as only jazzmen can in the presence of death. I sip a thimble of Irish Mist and watch from the balustrade as they pass beneath, the musicians in the lead, a coterie of little black boys dancing and strutting and imitating alongside and behind them. Followed by the pallbearers, the coffin, remnants of bereaved family, and then the public. A surprisingly large public.

At first I had panicked, fearing it might be him. Then I heard the sweet, mournful sounds, and knew he was still around to bid farewell to others. To fill the room with peace. A piano, they say it was. A piano from the Storyville days.

They will put him in a mausoleum. There is a curious fact about the dark New Orleans earth. It will not accept the dead. It vomits them back like unwanted chunks of meat, or asparagus.

It has to do with the humidity, I've read. And with the dampness of the earth, like an old cellar, and the proximity to the sea. Long ago, when they used to dig graves in cemeteries, the holes they dug would immediately, perversely, fill with water. The pallbearers would have to leap into the grave with pails and bail it out before the coffin could be lowered. Then they would have to stand on the coffin to keep it from floating to the surface, until enough heavy earth was shoveled in to hold it down. Even so, if a rainstorm occurred soon after, the coffin would rise to the surface through the muck.

166

Eventually they gave up. They began to build cemeteries above ground. Honeycombs of walls into which the bodies were put. (Like carbon copies one unaccountably keeps in a file, although certain they will not be needed again.) And for the well-off, of course, marble mausoleums.

This oddity, the dead refusing to stay buried, intrigues me. Corpses who would be God.

(Unlike him, in the dry desert sand.)

I didn't know his name. Nor does anyone. They never found his clothing, his wallet.

"John Doe," they called him.

I don't imagine that John Does resurrect.

Walter Briggs ▶

They never brought Jonesy back. I don't know what they did with him. They never brought him back. Instead that nasty guard Jackson came and put a cat in the cell across. A cat that as soon as it dropped to the floor on soft cat feet started to grow. A cat as big as a tiger. As big as an elephant. Its great green cat eyes staring through the bars across at me. Each eye as big as my head. The cat on its hind legs rearing up and gripping the bars with its two front paws and throwing its head back and its mouth open and meowing with a loud roaring meow as loud as a lion. Till Jackson comes holding Jonesy under his arm no bigger than a rag doll and throws him into the cage. And the great cat leaps and catches Jonesy in his mouth and swallows him in one gulp, without even chewing. Without a sound. Then the cat drops to all four legs and begins pacing back and forth inside the bars like the tigers we used to see at the zoo. I watch from behind my bars without a word. The cat sees me and rears up against the bars and rips the bars down with its paws. And comes across the corridor, this great cat lumbering toward me as fat as an elephant, this great cat elephant all black with a white head. And rears up on the bars and swipes at me as I pull back inside my cell, against the wall. The cat swipes again, leaning its giant weight against the bars, and the bars begin to rip from the ceiling where the dark stain is and I start to scream. I scream and scream and scream as the bars crash down and the cat starts coming toward me.

"Hey, Briggs."

The cat calling my name, its paw shaking my shoulder, only when I open my eyes there is a bright light shining and it's not the cat but the nice guard whose name I don't know. Holding a flashlight to my face.

"You all right?"

I wipe my eyes, my whole body shaking and wet. My heartbeat racing the sixty-yard dash in my chest.

"That must've been some nightmare," he says.

"Yeah," I say. "It was."

"You take it easy now," he says.

"Yeah," I say.

He goes out of the cell and locks the door behind and disappears down the corridor with his light. The cell is dark again.

In the dark I see the floor is covered with cat hairs. And Jackson's face peering around the corner through the bars.

Josephine Briggs ➤ Miss Sarah has a Bible in her

place. She took it down the other night when I asked. Me sitting in a rocking chair reading from the Psalms while she in a wing chair knitting. The thing she is knitting folded back and forth on the floor beside, bigger than a junkyard dog. Three feet tall of worry.

Read aloud, she said, and I did. From Psalms and Matthew and Job. Her knitting and me reading aloud. And in the daytime every day sitting together on the steps, holding signs. Sometimes people going up the steps stop by and say things of encouragement. For which we thank them. Other people say nasty things from far away. These we make believe we can't hear.

One day that lawyer lady came again and tole us not to give up hope. The Governor hasn't said no yet to the appeal, she said. As long as he doesn't say no there is hope.

She is a cute thing, that lawyer girl. She sure don't look like no lawyer, tall and expensive with cigars. But you can't tell nothing by looks. I remember that time the civil rights people arrest them Klan folks in Georgia. What a surprise it was under those hoods. Big smiling faces we did business with every day. Yes, ma'am, and no, ma'am.

Every day we sit on the steps with our signs. Then go to her place at night, shopping on the way. One day she cooks and I help. One day I cooks and she help. Salad, chicken, whatever. No big feasts exactly. Most nights we aren't too hungry.

Sometimes I worry about Leroy, home alone all this time. Why don't you call him, Miss Sarah says. It cost too much, I say. Don't be silly, she says. Call him now. I insist. So I do.

Leroy answers, all is fine, he says. Glum and speechless as usual. Saying yes and no and not much else. Cora is fine, he say when I ask. Angel is fine, he say when I ask. Then he say, Mama, and I say, yes, and he say, Mama, you going to call me if there is any good news? And I look at Miss Sarah and say of course I am. The minute there is news I will call. Even the last night, if it takes that long for good news. I will wait by the phone all night, he say, to hear the good news about Walter. There is tears in my eyes when I hang up the phone. About all those bad thoughts I thought.

Leroy is fine, I say to Miss Sarah, but I'm not exactly sure. There, doesn't that make you feel better, Miss Sarah says. I say it does.

I know who she is by now, of course. After all the people's remarks. I think about it a lot, but I don't say nothing. She don't mention it neither. I figure it is her business only, not mine. A woman leave her man after thirty years, that's nothing to do with Walter. Not really.

Simon W. Merton ➤ It's been raining steadily for days. The leaves outside the cabin window glistening gray under the bright sky. Moist as labia. (A simile inspired, no doubt, by my reading.) Any man who would leave his cabin in this pouring rain to stand in a stream and fish is a damn fool. So think the trout, and I've been dining well.

At night I've been reading Ernest Becker. *The Denial of Death.* A provocative work. Refuting Freud's claim that sexuality is the basis of all neurosis. It's man's inability to come to grips with his creatureliness, Becker says, that causes most of the problems. Man's mind can soar to the stars, can make him a philosopher. But at the other end he stinks, he shits. No matter how high he builds his throne, he still must sit on his ass. He is a creature like all the others. His shit smelling no better than the dogshit in the streets. Every man born, as someone said, between shit and piss. He is a creature like all the others, and he will die like all the others. Worse. *He is the only creature that knows it is going to die.* This knowledge is what man goes through life denying, avoiding, repressing. The knowledge of his personal doom. This repressed knowledge is at the heart of neurosis, Becker says.

It is food for plenty of thought. But surprisingly, in the chapter I am up to, he is beginning to lean toward religion as an answer. Not organized religion or blind faith. Not Sarah's kind of faith, the magical lighting of candles, the mystical murmuring of prayers. But a kind of *intelligent* faith. When one by one you strip away all of man's illusions, he says, you are left with the unity of nature, with the essentiality of an original creator. With God, if you will. Minus the beard and the toga. Approximately the same place Kierkegaard landed.

Intelligent faith is a contradiction, of course. It is in this contradiction, this gap, that modern man is wallowing. In which he might very well drown.

So says Becker. I think he may be right. I can see his answer, but I cannot feel it. Therein lies the problem.

I put the book aside and go to bed, the rain still drumming on the roof. I think of Walter Briggs. Trying to deny no longer at least his impending death. The truth is, I would not be unhappy if he was granted clemency. Twenty years to life, something like that.

I've never sent a man to his death before. But in this matter of clemency I am powerless.

It used to be up to the Board of Pardons. Now it is up to the Governor. The representative of the people.

Daralyn Kirk ➤ I wake up gray with my dress all clams like the window in Pinky's apartment after a bath. I fluff it out and start to walk and then I know it happened like I hoped. I have woke up smart.

I turn and walk away from the beach. Utah is across the sea but I know I can't just go across the sea. I got to go by car. Get rides by car and save my dollars to buy a gun in Utah. To get him free. I walk down streets and go behind a bush to pee and walk and walk till I come to the big fat road. And climb this rail and walk beside the road like that old time then when he stop with his jacket and his bike. And walk in the gray with the sun coming up and not too many cars till this great long silver truck with screeching fart pull off ahead and wave to me to come. And in it this man with glasses and silver hair and a long-sleeve shirt of red and black all over. Where you going, he say. Utah, I say. That's a mighty long way, he say. I guess it be, I say. Well, I can get you far as Memphis, he say. That be on toward Utah, I say. It's a start, he say. Hop in. So I do. He reach across and slam that heavy door and push his stick and that great big elephant truck fart more and we be on the road, the buildings on the side running back.

You sure are traveling light, he say. It's better than the dark, I say. He laugh. You look like you slept on the beach, he say. That's where I did, I say. You got your family in Utah, he say. My boyfriend, I say. We going to be married. He look at me scantwise from the side. You sure he's out there waiting for you, he say. I look at him scantwise back. What for did he say that? Of course he's out there waiting for me, I say. How's he gonna get out until I come? He look at me and don't say nothing and shrug his shoulders and drive. The sun warming up all over the window now. Drying out the clams.

You mind, I say. Mind what, he say. If I go to sleep, I say. I didn't sleep too much on the beach. Sure thing, he say. And reach behind his seat and pull a pillow. I put it behind my head but it don't stay. On the window, he say. Lean it on the window. I do what he say and put my head against it. It bump at first but then it's sleepy nice.

The truck screech wake me and I open my eyes and we is pulling off the road. Lunchtime, he say with the sun all bright overhead. By the way, he say, my name is Joe Glover, what's yours? Daralyn, I say. Not Daralyn Kirk Twenty-two Edgemere Miami. Just Daralyn. In case they be looking for me. I smile. The sleep has made me smart now again.

We go in this diner and sit in a booth and I go to the ladies' room. I do my stuff and wash my face and wipe it with paper towels. My hair all strings like a mess. On the side I see this machine what got a comb. I go to the lady and give a dollar and get four quarters back. I go on back and put a quarter in like them slut machines in Vegas. And push a button but out come not a comb but this little tube of stuff. I read on the label what it says. d-o-u-c-h-e. Dowchie. I don't know what it is. I put it in my pocket and make sure I press the button by the comb. And put a quarter in, and out a comb come. And see they got lipstick too for fifty cents, and get me one of those, and go to the mirror and comb my hair and put the lipstick on, and then put them both in my pocket. It cost a dollar but you want to get to Utah by car you got to look pretty all the time. That is what smart people do.

I go back out and he is got a hamburger half through and one there for me too. I eat it all quick and hungry and drink a soda pop. And him drinking coffee across. I take out a dollar to pay, but he say no, the treat's on him. For which I say thanks. I figure he will take his pay in other ways but that's okay with me. I need my dollars for the gun.

We go to the truck and drive on again, across the afternoon and into night. Lights bright by the road and stars above. With the radio on playing country music and him with a smile and a look in his eye that I know what is coming. I wait for him to stop by the road. But he don't stop he keep on driving ahead.

Been on the road for a week, he say, talking. Philly and Boston and New York, and back down to Miami. Now he on his way home to Memphis where his wife and kids. And smile when he say that. Both boys in high school, he say. Be playing football come fall. And smile again with that look in his eyes, and I see he is thinking about his wife, not me. Now that is a new one on you, Daralyn Kirk, I say to myself. That is a new one on me. And it makes me feel smiles all over.

Leroy Briggs ➤ I doan know what it was they did to Angel. I ain't seen her since. Though I can guess.

She never call. Every night I call her at her house. Every hour. Her mama answer every time. And hang up when I ask for Angel. Stop calling, Leroy Briggs, she say. Angel won't see you no more. You're no better than your brother.

Sheeet!

Finally I can't stand it no more. I got to see what it was they done to her. I walk across Gun Hill Road and on down to the tenements. The elevator broke as usual. The hallway smelling of broken wine and piss. And climb the three flights to her door. My bloodbeat pounding away as I ring the buzzer. Inside noisy feet come to the door. Her mother.

"Who is it?" she say without opening up.

"It's me."

"Who's me?" she say.

"Me. Leroy."

Sheeet! I eat dinner there a dozen, twenty times.

"We got nothin' to say to you," she say. "Go on home."

And hear the noisy footfeet walk away. I ring the buzzer again. Ring and ring until the feet come back. And unlocks a latch and the door opens a crack, her mother's eye peeking out.

"Scat," she say. "We doan want your kind around here no more. How dare you show your face here at all?"

"I want to see Angel," I say.

"Angel doan want to see you," she say.

I don't believe that. I don't believe one word of that at all.

"I just need to talk to her," I say. To explain.

"She doan want to talk to you," she say.

"Let her tell me that herself," I say. "If she tells me that I'll go."

"Anyway, Angel's not here," her mother say. "She's staying in Buffalo with her aunt."

"Why?" I say.

"Because I sent her there," she say.

I don't know if to believe her. I know she got an aunt in Buffalo. She used to go there summers as a girl. She tole me once. But I got this feeling she is right there in the house. Right there in her room, waiting for me. Wishing her mama wasn't home. I got this feeling I should push open the door right then. Push it in her mother's face and barge right in. And find Angel in her room and see what happened. But I know if I do then Angel will never forgive me. If I push past her mama then Angel won't see me again. So I hold myself back. My bloodbeat pounding in my chest.

"When's she coming back?" I say. Sounding polite.

"I doan know," her mother say. "For you maybe never."

And close the open crack and locks the latch.

I stand there like a fool. Wanting to kick the door. Wanting to kick it in till I hurts my leg. Kick it in like Walter did his locker.

Instead I walk away and down the steps.

At home I lie in bed and look at the wall. Wanting Angel to be there beside me. And get up 'cause I can't lie still. Wanting Angel.

Before I didn't know if I could do it.

Now I know.

Tit for tit.

That's the way the whole world works.

Belinda Marshall ➤ They sit on the steps like the

Two Fates waiting for their Sister. One white and one black, joined at the hip, it seems, as if they had been joined like that since time began, with the sun gleaming golden off the capitol dome behind them. One with graying hair and rimless eyeglasses, a spot of red where the glasses pinch her slim nose, a small brown mole on her chin below her lip, on the left side, a mole she must have hated to distraction in the mirrors of adolescence. The other with black hair and brown skin, a nose slightly flared but not exaggerated, matriarchal good looks preserved by prominent cheekbones that must have drawn plenty of beaux to the blacks-only dance halls of Georgia long ago.

Reading from the Bible, each to each, sitting on the marble steps under the deep blue sky, and passing it one to the other when throats go dry. The two of them a motionless rocky island in the swirl of people moving on Important Business past and around. Unable to affect the universe, though the round marble columns of power tower above. Looking like the Two Fates nonetheless, or like the progenitors of all mankind. The Mothers of Lost Sons, in war and peace. Mere symbols now, stage props, in the drama that is unfolding without their assistance, the drama they are powerless to resist.

Who am I, then? The missing Sister? No, I am too young, too unlined, for that. Though one day, who knows? Their daughter, perhaps. Their daughter in winter's slim boots and short skirts or summer's stylish dresses (stylish for Utah, anyway), their daughter braless under blouses on weekends (though at other times, of course, we must preserve the dignity of the court), their daughter who treads the marble halls herself, looks justice in the eye, reads in leather books other than the Bible; Portia with scales in one hand and a bloodied diaphragm in the other, their daughter who lost her virginity so long ago she cannot remember when (a lie) or to whom (another lie), who can scarcely count the number of men she has lain with (eight), who breaks some codes and argues for others, Daughter of the Fates, the New Woman, afraid in her heart of hearts that one day she may be one of them, a Mother of Lost Sons herself (or Lost Persons), afraid though her admiration for the two of them sitting there knows no limits. Daughter of woman and woman, white and black, conceived in some tender inviolate moment without the aid of man. In spite of man. The Two Fates begetting . . . what?

The overblown rhetoric of summation.

Female sexist diatribe.

But that lasted all of a week. Maybe less.

Jim is very nice. I've seen him several times.

Wade Pardington ➤ The procedure is simple, I'm told. You get to the prison before daybreak. The warden issues rifles, already loaded. You're not allowed to check the breech. In the yard they have a wooden chair set up, about ten feet in front of the wall. About thirty feet in front of that is a dark curtain suspended on a bar. Cut into the curtain are five rectangular holes, at the eye level of a man standing. You go out side by side and stand behind the curtain, so no one can see.

At the appointed time they bring him out into the yard. By then it is dawn, the light a brightening gray. The sun, when it breaks over the wall, illuminating the chair, not shining in the marksmen's eyes. If there is a clergyman present he utters a prayer, or gives the Last Rites of the Church.

The prisoner is permitted to make a last statement if he wants. Then a black hood is slipped over the upper half of his body. It covers his head and shoulders and chest. At the place on his chest where his heart would be a white circle is pinned to the hood. That is the target.

The prisoner is strapped to the chair. The clergyman and the guards move away. Each of us sights the rifle through one of the holes in the curtain.

When all is ready, the warden nods to the sergeant of the guards. The sergeant gives the command to fire.

At thirty feet it is almost impossible to miss.

The prisoner slumps in the chair. The prison doctor removes the hood and pronounces the prisoner dead.

You return the rifles to the guards. Five of you have fired

at the victim. But only four bullets have struck his chest. One of the rifles was loaded with a blank.

No one knows which rifle contained the blank. This is prescribed by law. So no man can be certain beyond doubt that he actually took part in the execution.

That part is a farce, of course. The kick is different. You can tell.

It seems sort of silly to me. We're all volunteers from the world outside: highway patrolmen, hardware-store owners, whatever. Chosen by the warden. The only requirement being that you can shoot. Anyone who is going to have a guilty conscience would not volunteer in the first place.

My view is that it's an unpleasant job. But there are lots of unpleasant jobs in society, and someone has got to do them. Unless we eradicate the vermin, decent folks won't be able to live.

The warden passed me over for the last one. He's got me scheduled for the one that's coming up.

Daralyn Kirk ➤ The sky is dark and dark with nothing but dark on the sides and nothing to tell what is out there whether houses or flat or what. The lights on the truck running on ahead of the truck, but the truck can't never catch up. And the wind whooshing in on the sides.

On and on we ride. Till far ahead on the ground there is a whole beach of stars. Twinkling on the ground. That's Memphis, Joe Glover say. My home town. And he take a deep breath and smile, like he is proud and glad to be home.

The stars get big and bigger as we come, and turn like magic into lights. Lights on streets and houses and stores and all, a whole big city full of lights. The end of the road, Joe Glover say and look at his watch. What're your plans, he say —I could come and sleep at his house though Ole Nance might be asleep by now and get scared when he walk in with some lady, but still it be okay if I want. No, I say, that would be nice but I got to keep moving on. Got to get to Utah in time. I don't say in time for what. I know Joe Glover wouldn't tell. Still it be smarter not to say.

Next exit is the depot Joe Glover say where he leave his truck and get his car and go home. If I want to get more rides then he better leave me here by the road. Okay, I say, and the truck screech fart and pull off the side of the road till it crunch to a stop. Well, good luck to you and to your boyfriend too, Joe Glover say and stick out his hand to shake. I stick out my hand and shake back. I don't remember anyone ever shake hands with me before. I like Joe Glover a lot, he is the nicest man ever. Almost as nice as him. I want to say something nice but don't know what. Then I think of what. Nice truck you

183

got, Joe Glover, I say. Joe Glover smile and wink. I could tell he liked what I said. Then he lean across and open the heavy door, and I say good-bye again and hop down. He lean across and close the heavy door tight and wave again. Then the truck screech up coughing gas that has a smell and he is gone.

I think to sleep on the side till it be light. Then I think if I get a ride I could sleep in there and get to Utah quicker. I walk along the road to get a ride. But it be night and not many cars. And them that do is coming fast and past me before they see me in the lights. It ain't no use. I walk away from the road till there is grass and curl up in the dark and go to sleep.

The dark is half past light when I get up. My dress all clams again, the grass all wet. I pee and straighten my dress and take that comb I bought from my pocket and pull it through my hair. Though I ain't got no mirror to see. And put new lipstick on, though I ain't got no mirror to see. You want to ride to Utah you got to look nice.

My belly is empty with hungry and I look around but don't see no place to eat. Only empty fields and that road rushing by across. Maybe I get a ride they will stop to eat. I go across the field, the hem of my dress hanging down where it is tore. I wish there was a nurse along to fix it. Somebody. But there ain't so I go across. The gray sky turning blue. Till I come to the road and over the little rail and walk beside, looking to the cars. They pass and pass and nobody wants to stop. Just pass and pass me by. Like nobody wants me at all. I walk and walk and nobody wants me at all. Till I feel I want to cry, which is no good. Like them nurses always said, it does no good. But still I want to until I think of him. Him who's out there waiting. Then I feel better, and I don't want to cry no more.

I walk and walk beside. Till this blue car pull off and stop ahead till I catch up. A lady and a man inside. I look inside and stare. They look like them. Like them that went away through the window, long ago. Are you them, I say. They don't answer. I say again, are you them? They look at each to each. Like they don't know if they is them.

You need a ride, the lady say. I say I do. Where you going, she say. Utah, I say. Utah, she say. Utah is west. We're going east, to Charlotte. Oh, I say. You want to go west you go on the other side, she say. Oh, I say. She smile at me but not as nice as Joe Glover smile. The car drive off.

I got to go across. I stand by the side and wait till all the cars. Then I run quick to the middle. And stand there on them bricks by this rail. And wait for all the cars. Then I think maybe she be wrong. She don't even know if they is them. How come she know about Utah?

I stand in the middle by the rail with the cars whooshing past on both sides and don't know which way to go. Maybe she is right and that is the way of Utah but I think she has said it wrong, it's the other way. If I be smart now then Utah is where I think.

Far behind the cars there is a truck. A big silver truck like Joe Glover's. The truckman will know the way is what I think. Truckmen know the way. The truck is coming bigger fast and won't stop with me in the middle. Anyone smart knows that. They only stop by the side. I got to run across very fast. So the truck will s

Virgil LeFontaine ➤ Death is all around me. Nothing has happened, and yet its fragrance is as enveloping as that of a fresh load of roses at the shop. Ever since that jazzman's funeral, death has lingered on, like some bittersweet tune from long ago. The kind of tune that makes you remember who you were with then, and what you were doing, and whether you were happy.

Happy. There is death in the very concept. Of all the words in the language, that is the most mortal.

I tell myself the impending death is the Briggs boy's, out there in Utah. But does that really have to do with me? The messenger?

I paste the picture in the ledger. The boy's mother, the judge's wife, protesting together. Executions make strange bedfellows.

On the way back from the bank I stop at Madame Eva's. An occultist. A fortune teller, if you will. A hundred years old if she is a day. Her coal-black face as craggy as the canyons of the West. Wrapped in a bright red cloak, a parody of a Storyville whore. Fortune's mistress.

She spreads the cards on a table and reads them under a dim hanging lamp that is swaying ominously in a sourceless breeze, casting liquid shadows on the walls. (Sometimes I think that I go through life trapped in Scenes already played. I do not know if that is universal or my own special fate.) She reads the cards with studied uncertainty.

"I see long life," she says. "I also see sudden death."

Equally practiced, I do not react. Offering no clues. She smiles with toothless purple gums.

"The long life is yours," she says. Thinking this will please me and earn her a larger tip. When still I fail to react, she frowns, like a bad actress.

"The death is someone close to you."

Her voice is hoarse as the desert. I want to hear more of it.

"That is not possible," I say. "There is no one close to me."

She looks up from the cards, warily, stiffly, as if her tired head will creak at the neck, like the door to some inner sanctum, and smiles slyly, as if she knows all.

"The death is not a loved one," she says. "It is someone you can touch."

She reaches across the table and pokes my shoulder with her crooked forefinger and cackles, her toothless mouth issuing the sound of rustled bones. She remains leaning forward, staring into my face. Her cloak slips off one shoulder, exposing a dark wrinkled breast shaped like a banana.

I give her two dollars for the reading and leave, the brightness outside assaulting my eyes without mercy. Irritated, I realize that she has unnerved me in spite of myself. Has forced me to acknowledge what I already knew. What my bones knew, and my blood, and the whorls of my fingerprints.

J——— is coming back.

Leroy Briggs ➤ I finish pumpin' gas for the day and go in the john and wash the dirt from my hands with Lava soap. The mechanic still working on some car. One day Mr. Hemus asked me if I wanted to be a mechanic and make more money. Sure, I said, who wouldn't want to make more money? He gave me a booklet to take home and read about being a mechanic. About how a car works. Be a good job, I figured, to know how a machine works. Then I looked at that book he gave me. All these words I don't know. Sentences I can't hardly read. They don't teach you to read good in school, how they expec' you to be a mechanic? Next day I tell him I changed my mind. I don't want to be no mechanic. I like it pumpin' gas.

Mama's face fell down when I tole her. What she expec'? She can read real good.

Crap to all of that.

I leave the garage and walk through the streets. Till I come to the one of the place where I will do it. Green lights down the block on both sides of the door. Across from them are little private houses that ain't no good. But a little ways up a tenement four floors high. I walk till I come to it and go inside. Two kids playing potsy in front. The hallways dark like every tenement is. I go up the stairs two at a time. Four floors. Passing no one. Till another stair leads to the roof, and I go on up and push open a metal door. And the sky hits my face on the roof. With nothing there but pipes standing up like midgets, and other roofs to see with midgets of their own, and around the corner the tops of trees in the street. I walk real

188

slow to the edge and lie down. A low brick wall at the end, to keep from falling. My eyes above the wall. And look down the block. Down into the street, where they will be.

It won't be no trouble at all.

Josephine Briggs ➤ I went to see him again in the prison. Him sitting there quiet and glum. More like Leroy than Walter. Not looking at my face but at the walls or down at the floor. As if my terrible wish come true.

I brought him Snickers again. He took them quick and put them in his lap under the table. As if he was ashamed. Saying that he was okay. That he would be free soon. Saying it in this faraway voice, like some prayer he didn't believe. And not much talk between us. As if some wall of brick has come between.

Walter who was always so playful. Like a puppy. Now it's like one they beat with sticks and stones. Still a puppy but he slink around with his head down and his tail between his legs. Waiting to be hit again.

I tole all this to Miss Sarah, sitting in the car. It's only natural, she say. Two years in a prison will do that to a boy. If only they would catch the real murderer and set Walter free, he would snap right back to his old self. You'll see. He'll snap right back, she say.

If only.

He act as if it is all my fault. I lie in bed in Miss Sarah's living room night after night and think that maybe he is right. Maybe it is all my fault. Maybe we should have lived in the South, like Harold wanted. And let him travel with the band like he wanted and come home every few weeks to see the boys. That's no way to raise children, I said. They got to see their daddy come home from work every night. So we move up North and Harold give up his music for the rugs. It work out fine and I know that I was right. And all the while whatever it was Harold blew out through his music is backing up in his blood. Till he go off nights and hang out with those jazzmen downtown. And start using stuff. To fill the hole in his soul where the music used to be. To make up for all the clapping and loving he wasn't getting any more. More and more stuff he use. Till there is no more money for me and the boys. Only for the stuff. Till he don't want the boys to see what is happening to their pa. And he leave. Leaving only good memories of their pa.

Maybe he was right. Maybe if we stay down South none of this would have happened. How's a body to know? How's a body to know what to do with kids? What to do with anyone?

Lord, I say, twisting Miss Sarah's white sheets between my fingers, Lord, if I made a mistake, You sure is punishing me real good.

Belinda Marshall ➤ Jim likes the early Bergman movies but not the later ones.

He likes chocolate ice cream better than vanilla.

He uses the byline James M. Barnes. His middle name is Mitchell. His mother called him Mitch. He never liked it. After she died he started using Jim.

He has read *Crime and Punishment* twice.

He wanted to be a baseball player. He played center field in high school in Seattle. In college he edited the Michigan *Daily News*.

He likes to sit with someone in the park on Sunday afternoons, or sprawl on the grass, and make up names and life histories for the bugs that go crawling by. He is very funny at it.

He won a National Headliner Award two years ago for exposing corruption in the county commission.

He would like to write a novel someday.

He never used chopsticks until I showed him how the other night.

The picture on his driver's license is a scream. Even worse than mine.

He doesn't know this, but I have begun singing to myself in the mirror each morning when I wash my face. I have never done that before.

This morning, after my shower, in the fog of moisture on the mirror, I wrote the name Barnes with my finger. Above it I wrote Belinda.

Just testing.

When the moisture evaporated, the tracing of the names remained visible. I rubbed them off with a tissue.

Belinda Barnes has a nice ring to it.

Whereas Belly Barnes sounds like a comic strip.

I would, of course, retain Marshall professionally.

I am reading a legal brief at the moment. I have just read the same sentence nine times. This has got to stop.

In less than four days Walter will be executed, unless the Governor grants clemency.

And Belinda, sweet Belinda, is falling in love.

God above, we are your masterworks.

Walter Briggs ➤ Each time, after they come, for
meals or bedcheck, after they go, after their footsteps have
vanished down the corridor, each time, when I know I am
alone, I reach into its hiding place and touch it. And I laugh.

She came!

Who would have believed she could do it?

Just like she said in her letter. She came and brought it with
her.

How did she get it past them?

I don't know.

All I know is that she did.

And I took it quick and hid it in my shirt.

And brought it back to the cell and hid it here. Where they
will not find it.

Until I am ready.

Until I decide how to use it.

Then.

Josephine Briggs ➤ Hour after hour, day after day, we sit there, me and her. Hour after hour, day after day, until eternity. The minutes creeping on forever, till you think the day will never end. And then it ends and we are back in her house and of a sudden it has all rushed by. Two weeks I been here already. More. Today be Friday and on Monday they will kill my son. Unless some miracle.

Night after night I ask what I'm doing here. I should be home with Leroy. My living son. Till I spit out the words and curse the very thought. Like a tree with roots I must stay, until I see what happens.

Her knitting is as big as a chair. I can't stand to see it no more. I'm sick of the Bible too, the Lord forgive, and set it aside. And watch her knitting grow. Why don't you knit something else, I say. Start another. I can't, she say. If I break the skein then someone sure will die. And keeps on knitting, and what can you say to that?

"You got something to drink?" I say. "I sure could use a drink."

She put the knitting aside without a word and get up and go inside, to her bedroom. And come back with a bottle of Scotch, half full. As if she been drinking inside, at night, after we go to bed. She go to the kitchen and take two water glasses and pour each one half full. Not even soda or ice. Half full. And give me one and swallow a swallow bigger than I can drink. And sit on a wooden chair, and motion me beside. As if our knitting and Bible chairs ain't no fit chairs for drinking.

The whiskey burns the belly. She tells me about her son. The same age as Walter when he die, she say. Twenty years old when he die. A lot like Walter too, she say. A lot. At first she went to the court from curious, she say. To see who could do such a murder in the park. And something about Walter fascinate her. Right away she knew he didn't do it. Right away. And even so there was something more about him. And every day she keep coming back. Till it hit her what it is. Walter reminds her of Larry, her boy who died. She tell it to her husband. That black boy reminds you of Larry, he say. Surely you're joking. But she wasn't joking, she say. There was something about him the same.

She swallow down her drink and pour some more. Her boy finish high school, she say. And think about college. College or the war over there. She want him to go to college, skip the war. Maybe the war be over when he get out. The boy not sure which to do. You go to the war, her husband tell him, you go to college after on the GI bill. You be a hero. You want to go in politics, which he thought maybe he did, you got to have a record in the war. You skip the war you never get elected.

She stop talking. I drink my drink and say nothing. She start in talking again. He never got elected, she say. He never even got to college. He went to war and two years later they send him home in a box. She couldn't even open the box to look at him. It wouldn't be a good idea, they tole her, to look at him.

I shake my head. Shake my head for her pain. For all God's pain. I be of the Mormon faith, she say. We not suppose to drink. In all my life I never touch a drink, she say. Till the day they brought my boy home in a box and say I couldn't even look at him.

She pour the last drops in my glass. More than I need. And go inside her bedroom and come out with another bottle, all full. I'm not a alcoholic, she say. Don't get the wrong idea. I just take a drink at night, before bed. It helps to relax. And opens the bottle and pours another drink. And takes a sip and gags and starts to cry. And puts the glass on a table, her tears running down. I go over and kneel beside her and hug her to me. She is pretty far gone by now. I stand her up, her wobbly on her feet, and walk her holding tight inside to her bed. And stretch her out on her bed and help her undress and get her nightgown on.

I turn off the light and go on back inside. To the knitting and the bottles on the table. One empty and one full, and who is to say which is worse. I think how Walter would look in a uniform. Walter was young for the war, but he would've look good. We got pictures of Harold in uniform, long ago. He look real sharp. But I can't see Walter carrying no gun. Walter's not the type to hurt someone. There's too much life in him for that. That's what's wrong with all of this. Walter couldn't hurt a soul. That's his mama talking. If a mama don't know her own boy, who does?

Walter Briggs ➤ Sometimes I think I will use it to kill Jackson. Stick it in his mouth and blow his head off. So he can't throw cats in my cell.

So they will have a real reason to do what they want to do. Instead of a false one.

Other times I think I will use it to escape. Grab Jackson around the neck when he opens the cell door. Hold it to the back of his head. March him down the corridor that way. Make them open the door at the end, or I will blow his head off. March across the yard that way, holding it to his head. Make them open every door and let me free. Or I will blow his head off.

The only question is when. When to do it.

Most times now the nice guard comes. Not Jackson.

The only question is when.

Belinda Marshall ➤ Saturday night./Panic night for the lonely./Dress-up night for lovers./Night of drunks and suicides./Night of soft hands on zippers./Night of neon and sirens./Night of amber and Debussy./Night of silent screaming./Night of mawkish poetry./Night that never comes for prisoners./Night never-ending.

I put down the pen, and go into the bathroom and brush my hair. I asked Jim to leave early, afterward. Thirty-six hours for Walter.

There is reason to hope. Jim pumped McPhee, the Governor's press secretary. Strictly off the record. He said the Governor is impressed with my brief. Has found some of the arguments persuasive. The circumstantial nature of the evidence. The fact that the Kirk girl recanted her testimony. He's beginning to think it's possible, just possible, they would be killing an innocent man. But he's not sure yet, in his own mind. It could hurt him politically. Could cost him re-election next year. He'd be tarred with "soft on crime." Half the state lives off tourists. Crime in the parks could wreck the economy.

Also, he's been mentioned as a possible Vice-Presidential candidate. A soft-on-crime image wouldn't help that, either.

But all that is irrelevant, McPhee assured Jim. (A smile on Jim's face.) The Governor will decide strictly on the merits of the case. He is sorely troubled by it. He has my brief on his desk and a copy of it at home. It could go right down to the wire, McPhee said.

Lord. As if it's a basketball game and not a boy's life in the balance.

All of a sudden we've begun to attract national attention.

199

A *New York Times* correspondent is here from Denver. She called me for information this afternoon. The Los Angeles *Times*, the Washington *Post*, and *Newsday* called long distance and are sending people out tomorrow. Jim says a camera crew from one of the networks showed up at the capitol today. He thinks the others will follow. Mom called while I was getting dressed and said the national news had mentioned it tonight. She was real excited.

I don't know how I feel about it. The media gets all worked up every time an execution approaches. But where are they in between, when the legislatures keep passing capital punishment bills?

There's only one way we'd have a decent criminal justice system in this country. If prisoners could vote.

I put down the brush, go to my dresser, open the top drawer, and pull out the postcard that came this morning. A picture of a beach on the Mediterranean, with a too-blue sky. And a message on the back. "Having a wonderful screw. Wish you were here." Postmarked Monaco. In his handwriting.

He had the nerve to sign it "Eric and Estelle." I guess that was the message. The star-crossed lovers, together again.

I tear the card in half and throw it in the basket. In the bathroom I brush my teeth. Raising the pink plastic cup, I look at myself in the mirror. I rinse a toast to them. To the happy couple.

I turn out the lights and slip under the sheet. On the night-table clock the numbers glow green.

Virgil LeFontaine ➤ The terrible, terrible dread has returned.

I don't know why it comes on certain days and not on all the others.

Perhaps it has to do with one's dreams of the night before.

I don't know why it usually comes on Sundays.

Perhaps because it is the Lord's day, and Vengeance is His.

The dread makes the cells of my blood quiver. It cleaves my brain from the inside of my skull, leaving a crawl space of air between, air that presses. It sets my hands to shaking, my eyes to back up with tears that will not fall, tears that are drained from the inside, till they water and dilute my soul. Inchworms of scream span synaptic gaps. The emptiness of life stretches out before me in an endless skein. And at its endless end the certainty of death, of burial in the earth. Of ants eating my flesh. Of worms boring into my eyes. (The reason I live here. Burial above ground.)

I drink drinks. I swallow pills. On these days nothing can still the dread.

I lie on the bed, half drugged, hoping it will pass. Desperate for it to pass. And listen to the music drifting in through the window. Hoping the music at least will rout the dread. But it is no use. The music is not the same. I strain my ears to listen, but there is no denying it. The horn is gone. The sweet mournful horn whose sadness I reveled in, whose pure pitch brought me peace, is missing. Perhaps he is merely late, I tell myself, and will be back for the next set. But there is silence, stippled with city noise, and longing. And then the music again. And still the horn is missing.

201

Perhaps it is a trick of my ears, I think. A nasty trick of the dread. Perhaps I should go down there, to see for myself. To that sweaty place of sweet sounds and body smells. And ask about the horn.

I rouse myself in the bed and swing my short legs to the floor. That's what I must do. Direct action. Direct confrontation. The only way to escape the dread.

I remove my robe and spray on deodorant. I put on a fresh shirt and my clean white suit. Battling the dread, I stand on the balustrade, tying my black bow tie, looking down over the Quarter. Neon lights moving impotently over the burlesque bars in the still-bright sun. Tourists with cameras like black hip goiters in the street. The girls in white boots on the corners. Somewhere out of sight the muddy river flowing that will outlive us all.

I turn and step inside. My knees go weak. I grab the doorjamb to keep from fainting. Cold sweat sullies my temples.

J——.

He is there, hovering near the ceiling.

His neck broken. As always. His dangling naked legs three feet above the floor.

Incorporeal vision that haunts me. Fountain of wisdom and humanity. Martyr and puppet both.

(Who pulls my strings.)

My submission to his will refines an adage. The sleep of reason produces not monsters, but masters.

Josephine Briggs ➤ Miss Marshall call and say there still be hope. That maybe the Governor will stop it. I know there still be hope. There always be hope as long as there is life. Else why would I be here?

We sit in a diner some miles along from the prison. Miss Sarah in the ladies' just now. Me sipping coffee. Not hungry for anything else. Soon we go back to the prison. To the warden's office, and meet Miss Marshall there. She talked to the warden, she said. We can wait there by his office through the evening. And on through the night if it take that long. So when the call come from the Governor we will hear about it right away. If the call come. When.

Of course there still be hope. I remember when Walter was just a baby, a little thing in his crib, with big brown eyes. Overnight one time he took sick, without no reason. A hundred-five fever he had, and the doctor don't know why. They took him to the hospital. Jacobi, across Pelham Parkway. They look him up and down and don't know why. They give him baths in ice, and shoot in penicillin, and lots of things to drink in his bottle. Nothing help. He lay there in his crib, all parched and hot. Two weeks he lay like that, and they don't know what to do. They 'fide it to Harold in the lobby, and I overhear. The fever don't break soon he die. And nothing that anyone can do, besides pray.

Next day the fever broke. The nurse come in and it was gone. As sudden as it came, and no reason. Two days later we took him home. He never been sick from it again. Whatever it was. The Lord just look down at him that time and save his life.

Miss Sarah come back from the ladies'. We finish our coffee and go on outside to drive back. Blue mountains rising all around. They sure put their prison in one pretty place. Only once you're inside you can't see it.

Me still all upset about before. They wouldn't let me see him.

I went to visiting hours, one more time. And wait in the room with the fence and the picnic bench. And wait and wait and Walter don't come. Then some guard come alone. He say Walter don't want to see me. He don't want to see no one.

"I'm not no one," I say. "I'm his mother."

"Sorry, ma'am," the guard say. "He just don't want to come. We can't force the men to see their visitors."

I sit with disbelief, not moving. Walter don't want to see me, his mother? On this, the day before? I sit there without what to say. All upset inside. The guard just standing there.

Then I think: there's something funny about how he's standing there. As if that guard got orders not to tell him I am there. Not to let me see him.

Why that be, I think. Why would they do that?

Then I tell myself, Josephine Briggs, don't start fooling yourself now. Don't make excuses and blame everyone else, just 'cause Walter won't see you. He must think it's better this way.

The thought brings tears I swallow. I got no use for people who 'sist on fooling themselves.

And then again I think, why won't they let me see him?

Simon W. Merton ► Refreshed in body and mind

after two weeks of fishing and reading. No man can spend time better. Food for the body and the soul.

I have no regrets as I pack the car and drive away from the cabin, along the rutted dirt road that winds down the mountain toward the highway. Tomorrow it will be over for Walter Briggs, one way or the other. A victim, I suppose, whether he is guilty or innocent. And yet his fate will not affect civilization; will touch his parents perhaps, but little else. His death, if it is to be his death, no more meaningful than the corpses of the flying grasshoppers splattering on the windshield, leaving streaky yellow stains. His life, if he is to live, no more meaningful than those of the grasshoppers that survive, to splatter on other windshields, other days.

His life or death no more meaningful, in fact, than mine, if I were to have a blowout now and go careening through the guardrail down the side of the cliff in flames. Who would regret it, once the simple ceremony was done?

And yet there is nothing we can do but stumble through the passing time from day to day, pretending that it matters.

It will be over with the Briggs boy tomorrow, one way or the other. But for me and Sarah nothing will have changed. How could it?

I can imagine the reactions of her friends (our friends?) when they heard that she had left me. How unlike her, they must have thought. How uncharacteristic. How impetuous. Not really knowing her. Knowing only how inertia had painted her. The stately court portrait covering over the woodland nymph. Nymph who insisted on dating others all

205

the time we courted. Who was pregnant before the wedding, and not by me.

I forgave her, of course. We would raise it as our own and have others besides. And then the terrible birth. The baby was fine, but the bleeding wouldn't stop. They had to take her insides out. There would be no more. There would be none of ours.

She never believed I could love Larry as much as if he were mine. I suppose we should have adopted, but that's hindsight. We were comfortable together. Until Larry was killed. Then she would sit there with a glass in her hand and sneak glances at me as I read the paper. As if it were my fault. As if I had sent him off to war to be killed. To punish her for some imagined crime.

Maybe it's best that she left. For the last ten years we've been pretending. The way most people do.

And yet, if we pretend, it is better to pretend together. I don't want to grow old alone.

Later, turning the key in the lock, opening the door, I have a vision of a pot roast simmering on the stove. A vision that she has returned. And neither of us will mention it again.

Inside, the house smells of must. It is as empty as when I left.

Belinda Marshall ➤ The clock on the wall in the warden's conference room has a large, open face. It reminds me of the clocks in elementary school that watched us wriggle on our little bottoms, impatient for the day to be through. Desperate for the time to pass. Desperate for milk and cookies, and freedom. Now we sit and stare at the clock, its hand large enough so that we can see the minutes jump, like nervous tics, and wait to see if the Governor will call. We are refugees from some black-and-white movie of the Forties, whose actors are long since dead.

The room and everything in it is cast, as if for the movie, in black and white, and somber tones of gray. The dark walnut conference table and chairs, the dark walnut benches along the wall, appear almost black under the white fluorescent lights. The walls are gray paint, the ceiling white paint, the floor a cheap gray carpet. The window high in the wall opposite the clock is black with night and lined with black iron bars reflecting thin lines of light. The three of us have all chosen to wear black for the evening, as if on the instruction of some unseen director, so that, prepared for the worst, we can celebrate the best. Even our complexions seem altered: Mrs. Briggs's face darker than usual, Mrs. Merton's face, my own hands, strangely pale and waxen. All of us mere backdrop for what we hope will be the bright red ringing of the phone.

The phone is on the desk in the warden's inner office, where he sits catching up on paperwork. He has been very nice about it, the door between the two rooms left open, so we will be able to hear the ringing. If it comes. None of us had the stomach to eat dinner before coming over, and now, as eleven o'clock approaches, he has sent a guard out for sandwiches and coffee before the diner closes down the road. They may yet go to waste.

I regret the arrangements. I thought it would be best to have us all wait it out together. To offer comfort together, or to celebrate together. Whichever. Now I think it was a mistake. We are together, but we are alone. There is nothing more to talk about. We sit silently, glancing each in her own impatience at the clock. Sometimes it has moved three minutes when I look. Sometimes two.

We sit haphazardly, the chairs pushed back from the table. Sometimes one or the other of us will stand, to pace, to relieve our muscles. Or to use the bathroom adjoining the outer office. Then return and sit for a time on one of the walnut benches.

I find myself wondering what Walter is thinking about, this night, in his cell. And cannot begin to imagine it.

I remember the day I first saw him, in the courtroom. The lost sheep. A day like any other. Ending now, two years later, with the clock ticking down toward his death. His execution. Ending now in this . . . this movie. This cheap suspense thriller. Except that it is not a movie. By the grace of law the state still murders people. It is real, and we are here. And the clock is moving.

I stand to pace about, and pass the open door to the warden's office. He beckons me inside and leans back in his chair.

"How you doing out there?" he says.

I think he is genuinely sympathetic. No decisions in the matter were his. He is not one of the old-line wardens. He is one of the new breed. Well-schooled. Compassionate. But trapped, like most of us, in a bureaucracy.

"Okay," I say. "As well as can be expected."

He nods. As if searching for something more to say.

"You should have been here for Gilmore," he says. "That was a real circus."

"Yes. I remember."

We look at each other, dumbly.

"If you need anything, just ask," he says.

I nod. He leans forward to his desk and picks up a folder.

I step out of his office, into the conference room. The clock has jumped two minutes more.

The women have moved, also. They are sitting together now, side by side, on one of the benches against the wall. Holding hands, their fingers entwined. The way lovers do. Or children.

Wade Pardington ➤ There are no special preparations the night before.

We had Virginia's mother over for Sunday dinner, as usual. Fried chicken and early corn. We drove her home and then watched TV after the boys went to bed.

The boys don't know about it. I was all for telling them, but Virginia said no. Time enough when they get older, she said. Maybe the world will change by then and such things won't be necessary. She's going to tell them I left early on a business trip.

I set the alarm for 4:30 a.m. Give me plenty of time to shave, dress, grab some coffee, and drive on out to the prison before daybreak.

When we got into bed and turned out the lights, I wanted to make love. But Virginia wasn't in the mood. I lay there and couldn't fall asleep. Finally I got my mind off it. Thought about the morning, and what I would wear. It sounds sort of silly, I know, but what do you wear to do something like that? A suit and tie?

Walter Briggs ➤ The nice guard comes into my cell

carrying a tray and puts it down on my bunk. Food is on the tray. On one plate a big steak, baked potato, lettuce and tomato. A hot fudge sundae in a tall dish beside.

"What's that?" I say.

"What you ordered," he says.

I don't remember ordering nothing. I ask the Prince of Horns. He didn't order it neither.

I shake my head. The guard shrugs and leaves the tray on the bunk and goes away.

The Prince of Horns looks at me sternly.

"Why didn't you do it then?" he says. "What are you, afraid?"

"I ain't not afraid," I say. "It wasn't the right time. The time has to be right."

"Right," the Prince of Horns says. And turns his back to me.

"Hey, what's the matter?" I say. "You angry with me?"

"I don't consort with chickens," the Prince of Horns says. And turns and looks out the window, into the yard.

I go and sit on my bunk. I feel it in its hiding place. Ready and waiting.

"Tomorrow," I say. "Tomorrow I will use it to be free. Or blow his head off trying."

"Talk is cheap," the Prince of Horns says, still looking out the window.

"Easy for you to be a big shot," I say.

Screw him, I think. And eat the hot fudge sundae that is starting to melt in the dish.

Halfway through it makes me sick.

I look at the steak and walk across to the bars,

"Hey, Jonesy," I say.

Jonesy don't answer.

"Hey, Jonesy," I say again. "You want to eat my steak?"

Jonesy don't answer. I turn and go back to my bunk. Outside the window it is dark. The cell lit by a bright bulb. The black stain I ain't seen for days.

Then Jonesy answers.

"Well, maybe I will."

I look across to see him. The cell across is dark. Then this black cat comes walking out of the cell, through the bars. It crosses the corridor. It steps over the bottom rung of the bars, its back arching like a snake. And walks into my cell.

I jump up from the bunk and back up against the wall, where the Prince of Horns just been. The cat leaps onto the bunk. It takes the big steak in its teeth and jumps down again, dragging the steak after it. Out of the cell it drags the steak, through the bars, into the corridor. And sits there in the corridor and starts to eat the steak. Paying me no mind.

I look around to show the Prince of Horns. I don't see him anywhere. Then something out the window catches my eye. I run to the window and grab the bars and look. In the night sky is a white stallion, a white stallion with wings, flying away over the walls. And on it the Prince of Horns. A golden crown on his head. His golden trumpet fixed to his saddle. In his raised right hand a gleaming sword.

"Hey, wait," I shout after him.

But the Prince of Horns is gone on his horse, away out of sight over the wall.

I stare at the dark sky, my body too heavy to stand. I slump down on the bunk, tired out. The Prince of Horns is gone and won't come back.

Later he comes on back, eating a hamburger.

Leroy Briggs ► In the corner of my room on the floor is this pile of dirty clothes. 'Cause there ain't no room in the hamper. 'Cause the hamper is taken. Every day after I finish pumpin' gas or after I eat dinner at Cora's and come home, I go first thing to the hamper and check it. In case they came back for it.

But they never did.

I go and get it now, flower box and all, and take it out of the hamper.

'Cause tomorrow they gonna waste Walter.

And if they do they got to pay.

I sit on the couch in the living room and check it out. The handle feeling good in the hands, like a good stickball stick. The TV rolling around, cutting off heads. I sight down the barrel at the TV screen, right between the eyes. Cutting off heads.

Walter was the best at stickball. Used to pitch sidearm, stepping toward third. Make everyone bail out.

Used to.

I look at the telephone black and quiet on the table near the couch.

Angel used to be my friend.

I take out the box of shells and load it up.

The clock is on the wall in the kitchen. Way past midnight already. I go to Mama's room for the alarm. And set it for seven in the morning. If Mama not call by then, then it be done.

I put the clock on the floor beside the couch. And stretch out on the couch in my clothes, near the phone. So I doan miss the phone if it ring.

If I can sleep.

They wait this long I doan think it's gonna ring.

Josephine Briggs ➤ On the big dark table is sandwiches half ate and coffee half drank in paper cups that taste like wax. Two bites was all I could swallow. Three hours is all that is left. All night we been here and it feel like a cemetery, waiting for someone to rise. Like we did one night when we was kids. All night we waited that time, from the stories we heard. But nobody ever rised.

The clock on the wall jump minutes at a time. Each jump a jump in my heart.

Me and Miss Sarah take turns walking around. Or sit on the bench together holding hands. Hands filmed with sweat from the holding. Black sweat and white sweat. A time like this the sweat is all the same. Down the other end of the table Miss Marshall sits, her elbows on the table, her head in her hands. Her eyes red from tired, and from crying in the ladies', I think, when we can't see. Her hair all mussed and not so pretty now. Sometimes holding hands with herself, her hands all pale from squeezing.

A few hours back I thought she would faint. I thought we all would faint. The time the telephone rang. Hour after hour we sit here, waiting for only one thing. Waiting for the telephone to ring. And then it rang and scared us near to death. Hearts racing like when the telephone rings and wakes you up in the middle of the night, and you get all scared 'cause you know someone is dead. And you reach to answer it and pick it up, and there is only breathing. Or a click of hanging up. And you left with your heart in your hands, and hours after can't fall asleep again.

We all sit stark up straight when the telephone rang. And

look at each other's faces each to each. Miss Marshall jump up from her chair and run around the table to the warden's open door and stands there listening. Me right behind her, and then Miss Sarah. The warden with the phone at his ear looks up and sees us in the door. And shakes his head from side to side. Shaking his head to say no. I felt my knees go buckle. I mistook what he meant. I thought he meant the Governor say no. I know that's not what Miss Marshall tole me before. She say if the Governor call then Walter's life be spared. If it not be spared then the Governor won't call. He won't call to say no. And now the warden shaking his head no and for a time I didn't understand. Then he hung up quick, looking all embarrassed and ashamed.

"I'm sorry," he said, looking us in the eye. "It was my son. He won't call again."

The deflate go out of us then. I think Miss Marshall would have fall to the floor if she wasn't holding on. We slump back to our seats like it is over. Miss Marshall go to the ladies'. She come back a long time later, her eyes all red.

All that hours ago. And the telephone not ring since. Hours of watching the minute hand go bump.

I think of Walter lying in his cell. I hope they give him something good to sleep.

I look up at the clock. I ask Miss Marshall out loud what time it be. She look down at the tiny gold watch on her wrist. Ain't none of us trust that big ole clock on the wall.

"Four-thirty," she say.

Two and a half hours.

Miss Sarah has got her eyes closed in her chair. Her lips moving to herself. I don't know if she is praying or is wishing for a drink. Maybe both.

Ain't no drink strong enough to make us feel good now.

Nor no prayer, neither.

Wade Pardington ► The clock-radio woke me at

four-thirty. The farm report. I turned it off quickly. Virginia stirred briefly but didn't wake.

I dressed as I had decided, in Levi's and a plaid shirt, and carried my hunting jacket downstairs. Outside the kitchen window it was still dark. The birds had not yet stirred.

I thought of fixing a big breakfast, but decided against it. Juice and coffee was enough.

Faint light was just beginning to appear in the eastern sky when I climbed into the pickup. It took a while to get it started. It needs a tune-up, but I've been putting it off. Truth is I could use a new truck. But they're so expensive nowadays, who can afford it? You've got to keep them running as long as you can.

Finally the engine turned over and warmed up in the cold morning air. I switched on the headlights and drove on out, heading toward the highway.

Somewhere in the vicinity, four other men I didn't know were also driving toward the prison through the dark. To do their duty.

Walter Briggs ➤ I lie on my bunk, staring up at the dark. The Prince of Horns kneels by the side of the bed, praying like he did as a child.

> Now I lay me down to sleep,
> I pray the Lord my soul to keep,
> But if I die before I wake,
> Pop goes the weasel.

My empty body lying in the bunk. The Prince of Horns all dressed in robes, with his crown of gold on his head.

My hand squeezing to powder this pill they give me to take. This poison.

> Now I lay me down to sleep,
> I pray my mama not to weep,
> The Prince of Horns he is a fake,
> Pop is a weasel.

Leroy Briggs ➤ Walter is dead.

Walter my brother is dead.

The alarm clock wake me from a dream. I jump up off of the couch and look at it. Five minutes after seven. I run into the kitchen and look at the clock on the wall. Four minutes after seven.

And Mama not called to wake me.

My hands start to shake a little. The anger backing up in my chest, like the water backs up in the sink. They do these things on the dot, that's what they say. They have gone and shot Walter dead.

The anger rise in my throat. Kill Whitey. That's what they used to shout when I was little. Me not knowing why.

Now it is pounding in my head. Kill Whitey.

I got to calm down. Got to take my time. Not get there too soon.

I go to the bathroom and splash cole water on my face. And wipe it on a dirty towel. Hot tears forming in my eyes. And wipe them again. I go to open the fridge and drink some orange juice from the jar.

I pace up and down, this angry blood in my blood. Kill Whitey, it say in my brain. And then this other, in between. Walter, I love you, it says.

I never said it out loud. Never even thought it before.

Walter, my big brother, I love you.

And go in the bathroom and wash my face again.

My clothes are all messy from being slept in. I go in and change my shirt. Put my sweat shirt on. Without thinking why.

219

The clock say seven-twenty-five.

In the living room the rifle is on the floor. I kneel down and put it in the box and wrap the tissue around. And close the box and tie that green ribbon around. Just the way it been. Like flowers.

The alarm clock ticking like a bomb. Kill Whitey.

I stand up and look around the room. This room I might never see no more. I think to write a note to Mama. A note of good-bye. But I know I can't write too good. And what is there to say?

I go and look out the window, down into the street. The sun beginning to shine. People in the street, going off to work.

I forgot to tell Mr. Hemus I wouldn't be in to pump no gas today.

Ain't no matter now.

I go and pick up the box, heavier than it looks. And on down the stairs, and close the door behind.

I walk through the streets, on toward the station house. Thinking that everyone I see is looking at me. Knowing it can't be true. Flowers is all I got. Is all they see.

On through the streets. Eight blocks, and turn left. And there it is, at the other end of the street. Green lights on each side of the door.

I cross the street and go to the tenement. People going out to work.

"'Scuse me," I say, carrying my box through the door.

They go on out right past.

Inside from the street it is dark. I climb up the stairs with my box. Passing some girl going down. All spiffed up for work, and smelling of perfume. Her teeth a sweet smile as we pass.

Up another stairs I go, and then another. And one more to the roof. Wondering which floor that sweet-smile girl live on.

I push open the door to the roof. Just a crack. And look around.

Ain't nobody on the roof. Just them midget pipes.

I open up more and step on out. And close the door behind.

Real slow I walk toward the edge. And stop a few steps before, and kneel down and put the box on the floor. And shove it toward the wall at the edge. And crawl on my hands and knees on after it.

I lie on my belly all quiet and shaking at once. And look on over the edge. The steps of the station empty. Must be a few minutes left. And open the box as if to take out flowers. Flowers for that sweet-smile girl.

The rifle smooth and heavy in my hands.

I lie on my belly and wait. Peeking every minute over the top.

And then they come.

The doors swing open and they start coming out. The eight o'clock shift, all dressed in blue.

I set up on my knees, the rifle leaning on the wall. They can't see me up here, all unsuspecting. But I can see them fine. Their faces big as pumpkins through the scope. Milling about and joking on the steps. From one face to the other I move the scope. Picking out which to be first. Big pink Irish faces, yellow Italian ones, Jewish ones. Skipping the blacks. O'Briens and O'Connors and stuff. Ready to move out with their nightsticks and bullets and guns.

I got to pick out one. One to start. I stop the scope and it is fine. Big and pink with light blue eyes. A regular pig's face.

I line him up good.

This be for you, Walter, I say under my breath.

This be for you.

Virgil LeFontaine ➤ Human contact, fraught as it
is with danger, sometimes palliates. Temporarily dilutes the
dread with the illusion that it is possible to escape from one-
self. From the self-devouring monster that dwells like a tapeworm within. The tapeworm we love to hate. And love even
more to feed.

Seeking escape, curious to the point of bravado, casual as
a man-about-town, I slunk past him last night (he is patient
with me, he knows I always return) and slipped down into the
street, moved through the Sunday night throngs, to that vul-
gar place whose drifting music enchants. Paid the dollar ad-
mission, stepped in (dived in holding my nose?) to the en-
gulfing sea of the jazz. Human thighs pressed each to each in
the small wooden grandstand. Hands clapping, toes tapping,
heads bobbing, all the spectators trying desperately to pene-
trate the music. As if it were a woman. (A spectator at life,
I never harbored such illusions. Never fostered the possibility. I suppose that is my curse. To have been born a realist.)
I found a stool at the bar in the amber smoke and ordered
bourbon. (I detest it, I did not drink it, but it is all that bar-
keeps respect.) Sometime after he set it down, during a break
in the music, I caught his eye.

"New man on trumpet," I said. With the casual air of a
regular, which of course I am, unknown to him, up there on
my balustrade. (My keen ear hardly necessary here, where
the new man had been blasting and strident, instead of sweet,
mournful, accepting.)

The barkeep merely nodded.

"What happened to the other fellow?"

"Quit to go up North. You know these cats. Always on the move."

I pretended to sip the bourbon. The glass itself smelling of hospitals.

"Pity. He was one sweet horn." The words sounding forced in my voice.

"He could make you cry," the barkeep said.

Offhandedly. A turn of phrase. Not meaning it.

Then he was gone, down the bar. The music blasting again. I tipped him lavishly, out of guilt for not drinking the bourbon. And slipped out of the smoke into the humid street, past ovals of flesh, back to the apartment. Where I knew he would still be hovering, insistent.

Belinda Marshall ➤ They are going to kill Walter

at seven. It is now five minutes to six. The hands of the clock at once racing like wild stallions and dragging huge blocks of cement.

I thought our nerves would be strung like high-tension wires, but we have slumped beyond that. All of us have gone limp in our chairs, collapsed in postures of despair. Even the warden, who I can see through the open doorway, has thrown his head back and closed his eyes, trying to catch a nap or unable to fight it off.

I find my mind wandering the way it does at concerts, unable to concentrate for long periods on the music. Thinking of Jim, wishing he were here now, offering a shoulder to doze on. Thinking of calling him from the pay phone in the hall, but I don't want to wake him. He had offered to come and sit here through the night. I told him no. Still, his presence in the city, his presence in my life, seem now like a safety net. However this dread night ends, he will be there to prevent me from crashing to the jagged rocks below.

And then this other thought that has not yet been spoken between us except with the sparkle of our eyes. That if all goes well, October weddings are nice.

I interrupt the train of my thoughts, feeling guilty. I am sorry, Walter. . . . But if evil thoughts, as opposed to deeds, not be evil, how bad can good thoughts be?

My mind babbles on with exhaustion. Clear streams and muddy ones mingling. The clock two minutes past six. And if my mind is foggy, what of them, slumped across the room?

Too frayed and empty now even to hold hands any more. What are . . .

I don't believe it.

I dare not.

Silence again. As if it were the wishing of a dream.

And then again. A ringing.

Can it be? That he waited this long to decide?

Through the open door the warden, rubbing his face with one hand, is reaching for the phone with the other. Not his son, dear God. Not again. Run to the door, Belinda Marshall, I tell myself, run to the door. My body obeys but in its own sweet time. Dragging its own cement blocks. While the two women, dazed and uncertain whether they heard correctly, follow even more slowly than me. No longer the Two Fates, but two frail ladies waiting for the word from on high.

The warden has the phone at his ear.

"Yes. This is he."

Who? Not looking up in our direction.

"Yes." Nodding to himself. "Yes, I understand."

And then looking up at us over the mouthpiece suppressing and yet not suppressing a smile and nodding to me, to us, nodding vigorously, while continuing to listen.

"Thank God!" I say aloud.

The two women beside me not yet certain what has happened, and I hug Mrs. Briggs around and kiss her firmly on the cheek, half leaning on her, realizing she is the one who should be leaning on me.

It's off, I want to say, the execution is off, but then I check myself. To wait till the warden says it. Maybe there is some option I never thought of. Some kind of delay without clemency.

I hold my tongue as the warden listens and talks.

"Yes, I understand, Governor. No trouble at all. I'll be sure to tell her. Right. You get some sleep too."

And then he hangs up and the grin breaks full on his face, like a moon peeping over a mountain.

"Sentence commuted," he says in our direction, loud and clear. "Twenty years to life."

We hug each other, the three of us together, hugging or holding each other up while the tears run down our faces. As if he were free. Knowing he will not go free. I choke the words out as clearly as I can.

"Seven years," I tell Mrs. Briggs, enunciating clearly through asthmatic breath, as if I were talking to a deaf person or a child. "He'll be eligible for parole in seven years. Five if you count time served. He can get out in five years. He'll only be what then? Twenty-five."

Mrs. Briggs composing herself, like the lady she is. Wiping away her tears. And smiling.

"He'll still be a baby," she says. "With a whole life to live."

Mrs. Briggs and Mrs. Merton hug each other again. The warden comes around from behind his desk and shakes hands with each of us.

"I just want you to know," he says to Mrs. Briggs, "that this was not a task I was looking forward to. I'm very happy it turned out this way."

Mrs. Briggs nods and thanks him. To me he says, "The Governor will have the papers on your desk first thing in the morning."

He goes back to his desk and picks up the phone again.

"I'll have them bring Walter up now," he says. "So you can all share the good news."

I coax Mrs. Briggs into a chair, while the warden dials the cell block. But in a minute she jumps up again.

"Leroy!" she says. "I got to call Leroy at home and tell him the good news." She opens her purse. "Has anyone got quarters for long distance?"

The warden stretches his phone across the desk.

"Here, use this," he says. "I think the state can afford it. Under the circumstances."

Josephine Briggs ➤ Thank the Lord, I keep saying to myself under my breath. Thank the blessed Lord. Five years in prison a long time for something he didn't do. But they ain't gonna kill him. They ain't gonna kill my Walter.

Miss Marshall sit me in a chair, but I can't sit still. The excitement jumping inside me. Excitement and joy.

"Leroy!" I say. "I got to call Leroy at home and tell him the good news."

I don't have quarters for the phone. The warden stretch his phone across the desk and say I can use that. Dial one and then the area code, he say.

I dial one, then two, one, two, and then our number. Clicking and static on the line. Then quiet. Then the phone start ringing. Another ring. Again. Again. Why don't Leroy answer? Another ring. Again. And still he don't pick it up.

I hang up the phone.

"He don't answer," I say.

The warden comes around the desk.

"Let me try," he says. "What's the number?"

I tell him the number and he writes it down. Then he picks it up and dials it all. And hands me the phone when it rings.

It rings. And rings. And rings. And still that boy don't answer.

I wait a few more rings. Then I hang it up.

"I doan know where he could be," I say. "He know it was set for seven. He said he would stay by the phone."

Miss Marshall look at me then with a wide face.

"It's after eight in New York," she say. "It's two hours earlier here."

I feel like a dumb fool. I plumb forgot to tell Leroy that. I half forgot myself.

"He must've gone out already," I say. "He must be on his way to pumpin' gas."

I go away from the phone and sit again.

"We'll call him again later," Miss Sarah say.

I look up at her and smile. She squeeze my hand.

Again I can't sit still. But I'm too tired to stand. High in the wall is a window with iron bars. Behind it gray light beginning to peek.

We all sit in chairs and wait for Walter. For reunion. A moment for a life. To have my son again. Without death. That is the center of being for a mother. As every mother knows. Things from the past run jumping through my eyes, all disconnected. About Harold and Walter and Leroy. About us. The Briggs family. What does the Lord think of us, looking down? Ain't no way to know. If I could see Him I tell Him one thing only. We try. That's all a body can do on this earth. We try our best.

I bring my thoughts down and look at the others. Miss Sarah with her eyes closed, a smile on her face. The warden straightening his tie that he had loosened. Miss Marshall I catch looking at my face. Her expression I can't make out. I look at her eyes, wishing she could read what was in my heart.

"Thank you," I say across to her, softly.

She smiles a small smile and winks at me.

My heart fills up with love for this girl. I think maybe she could read it after all.

I look down at my hands, all gnarled and sweaty. And then there is noises in the halls, noises of doors and footsteps. And the door opens and Walter steps in, in the blue denims they wear, with a guard stepping behind him. I get up from my chair and rush to him and throw my arms around him and hug my boy.

He doesn't hug me back.

I step back and look around, from one to the other.

"Doesn't he know yet?" I say.

The guard nods.

"He knows," the warden says. "The guard told him on the way."

I look at Walter. He hasn't said a thing. His face is smiling but a distant look in his eyes.

"Aren't you happy?" I say.

He nods his head.

He nods his head but something is wrong, and I don't know what it is. I don't know what it is but I want to scream.

Miss Marshall comes over and takes my hand and talks to him.

"Do you understand what happened?" she says.

"I'm glad I didn't do it," Walter says.

Miss Marshall takes Walter's hand too.

"We know you didn't do it," she says. "We've always known that."

Walter nods his head. My mind is playing tricks, I think. The look on his face is like he is ten years old.

"I didn't kill Jackson," he says. "I didn't kill Jackson with my gun."

The warden, listening from behind, comes closer.

"What gun?" he says.

"My gun," Walter says. "The gun that Daralyn brought."

I don't know what is going on. I look from one to the other. The words going back like Ping-Pong. I don't understand.

Walter turns to the guard.

"Tell him, Jackson," he says. "Tell him I didn't kill you."

The guard looks blank and shrugs his shoulders. I catch the warden's face. He is biting his lip. Miss Sarah is sitting down again, with her head in her hands. Miss Marshall's face is what my own must be. A mirror. Her eyes wide, her muscles tight. As if she wants to scream.

The warden looks at both of us. Saying words dry, words he don't want to say.

"This guard is not Jackson," he says. He is talking to me and Miss Marshall, not to Walter. "Jackson was fired several weeks ago. If Daralyn is Daralyn Kirk, she has never been inside these walls."

I listen to his words. I don't understand. What's all that to do with Walter? My mind not catching up.

The warden looks at Walter. He speaks both firm and soft.

"Do you still have the gun?"

Walter nods his head, like a little boy.

"May I have it?" the warden says.

Walter puts his hand in his pocket, and pulls it out. My heart cries out as I look. The paper wrapping is torn. The chocolate is melting: is oozing out all sticky in his hand.

Leroy Briggs ➤ I lie on the roof on my back and look
up at the sun. And close my eyes against it, the whole world
turning orange. And tears running down. And the rifle there
at my side.

Unused. 'Cause I couldn't do it.

Hot tears running down, ashamed. What would Walter
say?

Face to face to face I moved the scope. Picking out the one.
Right between the eyes I aimed it. Right between the eyes.

My hands shaking all over.

And for a second couldn't get it to work. The safety catch
stuck or something. 'Cause I never used a rifle before. And
pulled and twisted till it come unstuck. In plenty of time. Ain't
no excuse. In plenty of time to use it.

And then I couldn't squeeze.

Till they stop laughing and move on, out to patrol their
beats. And the rifle pointing down at empty steps. The tears
running down, the trigger still not squeezed.

Nobody knowing how close they come. O'Brien, O'Connor,
whoever.

Be home to see their little kiddies tonight.

'Cause Leroy Briggs is a chicken.

I lie on the roof on my back, flat out tired in the sun. Le Roi
Briggs. A turkey who is a chicken.

And cry and cry 'cause what would Walter say. Walter who
is dead.

And then in my orange eyes I see Walter. His face inside
my eyes, talking to me. Talking like he always used to do.

Hey, jerkhole, he say. What you crying for? 'Cause you

231

couldn't shoot those cops? That's real smart, boy. Shoot some cops and get yourself killed in return. A real bright plan. They swarm all over the street. They creep up over the roofs. Maybe they send a helicopter up. And shoot you down like a dog, there on the roof. That do me a whole lot of good, Walter say, orange in my eyes. It do our mama a whole lot of good. My baby brother splattered on the roof.

Then I hear other voices. People inside the door to the roof. I jump up and put the rifle back in the box. And cover the box up quick. And leave it there by the wall and hurry toward the door. And get there just as two fat ladies open it, baskets of wash in their hands. Coming up to hang out the wash.

"Morning," I say, stepping through the door.

"Morning," they say. And I go down the steps, and trailing behind is one of their voices saying, "Hey, son, you forgot your box."

And down I go down the steps, two at a time, and out into the street. And hurry around the corner. And walk and walk, every which way, an hour and then another, all kinds of things in my head. Till my breath slow down at last, and I go on home.

Up the steps I open the door with my key. The telephone there at the end of the couch is ringing.

Josephine Briggs ➤ They took Walter out of the prison in the morning. Miss Marshall got that judge to sign a paper. They put him in the hospital instead.

"He'll be better off there," Miss Marshall say.

Maybe.

"That hospital got bars on the windows?" I say.

Miss Marshall look down and say she guess it does.

In the afternoon we drive on out to see him. The three of us in Miss Sarah's car, 'cause Miss Marshall's not big enough. The hospital pretty enough for what it is, with white-painted buildings and green lawns and flowers lining the walks. We talk to the nurse at the desk, to get to see Walter in his room. They won't let us in. The doctors feel it would be better, she say, if they examine him first a week or two. He can't have visitors till then.

We look each to each. Ain't nothin' we can do. We go outside and sit on a bench across, too tired to walk to the car. Ain't none of us been to bed since yesterday morning.

The building standing tall across. In some of the windows are faces, looking out. I can't tell if any of them is him.

We sit on the bench all quiet. There don't be nothing to say. I take out a handkerchief from my purse and squeeze it tight. Miss Marshall I think is holding back tears. Miss Sarah reach into her shopping bag and take out needles and a ball of wool and start to knit again. A new one this time, the long black thing ain't with her. A maroon ball of yarn, and start to knit. The first line creeping across the needle looking like stitches on a wound.

"What are you knitting now?" I say, without thinking.

233

"I think maybe a scarf," she say.

I think of Leroy at home. I got him on the phone before we left and told him Walter was saved. At first he didn't believe me. Not till I swore on the Bible that it was true.

I didn't tell him about the hospital. Time enough to explain that later.

After a time we pick ourselves up and walk on back to the car and drive on back to town. Me in the front with Miss Sarah. Miss Marshall in the back.

"What will you be doing now?" Miss Sarah say.

Go on home, I say. Back to the Bronx. To Leroy. Back to work. Can't let my ladies die of dirty house.

"I just want you to know," Miss Sarah say, "that every chance I get I will come on out here and visit a bit with Walter. And write you letters telling how he is."

"I plan to come out too, as often as I can," Miss Marshall say.

I squeeze their hands and thank them with my heart. I know they both be sincere.

Won't be their fault they won't find the time, once the time comes. That's just the way it is.

Virgil LeFontaine ➤ J—— has spoken.

I know what I must do.

No more foul-ups. Not like the last time.

He explained the problem to me. It was the weapon. The knife was too big, and clumsy. They couldn't read it.

I will use something smaller this time. (I have already decided what. The scissors at the bank. I will steal them tomorrow, during lunch.)

Also, I must use capital letters, not small ones.

So there will be no confusion.

So they will not mistake the "o" and the "e" for periods.

So the whole world will read our message of LOVE.